MISSION OF MURDER

The tranquillizer drug Ameytheline was considered so safe that it was even prescribed for children, but it had deadly after effects. There was an antidote, but it existed only in the hands of a callous blackmailer who held the British Government to ransom. One of the faceless men of Whitehall revealed the facts to his most ruthless agent. And Simon Larren quietly left for Greece to steal the antidote and eliminate the man who held the lives of thousands in his hands.

ROBERT CHARLES

MISSION OF MURDER

Complete and Unabridged

LINFORD
Leicester

First published in Great Britain

First Linford Edition
published 1998

British Library CIP Data

Charles, Robert, *1938* –
    Mission of murder.—Large print ed.—
Linford mystery library
    1. Detective and mystery stories
    2. Large type books
    I. Title
    823.9'14 [F]

ISBN 0–7089–5221–6

Published by
F. A. Thorpe (Publishing) Ltd.
Anstey, Leicestershire

Set by Words & Graphics Ltd.
Anstey, Leicestershire
Printed and bound in Great Britain by
T. J. International Ltd., Padstow, Cornwall

This book is printed on acid-free paper

1

The Red Death

The child was dying. The two men by her bedside were grim-faced and helpless. The mother cried without noise, silent tears burning down her face and deep sobs moving convulsively in her throat.

It was a small room with a small bed, and the tiny form coughing out her life beneath the white sheets was smaller still. The rabbits and birds on the shadowed wallpaper were dim and subdued and a few bright comics and a large doll lay unheeded by the bed. It was many days since they had last been handled. The curtains were drawn and the light was filtered, but the ugly red blotches still showed up clearly on the little girl's sunken cheeks. She was paralysed from the chest down but one hand still moved feebly above the counterpane. The vivid red rash was again evident upon the backs of the tiny fingers.

The short, paunchy little man who was known in Whitehall as Mr. Smith laid a steadying hand upon his sister's arm without taking his eyes from the bed. There was a constriction around his chest, a feeling of bitter frustration, deep pain, and above all a sense of trapped and savage fury.

There was no need for this. *He* could have stopped it. Give the right order to the right man and *he* could have stopped it. It was too late now for the child on the bed — but there would soon be others.

He tried to clamp down on his thoughts, for there was nothing to be gained from condemning himself because of what he might have done. They had refused to let him do anything. The official voice had said no and he was forbidden to act. His hands were tied and all he could do was hold his sister's arm and try to comfort her while her daughter died.

The child burst into another fit of rasping coughing. The woman's sobs became audible. The doctor moved closer to the bed, his stooped shoulders obscuring their vision.

The coughing became more violent, more heart-rending — and then stopped. There was a long silence while the doctor examined his tiny patient, and then he turned to face them, straightening his shoulders wearily.

He said gently. "It's all over, Mrs. Taylor. She won't feel any more pain now."

Joan Taylor broke down into hysterical weeping. Her husband had died in a road accident six months before, and the still form on the bed had been her only child. Smith did his clumsy best to comfort her but only once in the next few hours did her words take any coherent form.

"Somebody must be able to do something," she said dully. "There'll be other little girls. *Somebody must be able to do something.*"

★ ★ ★

3

It was mid-afternoon when Smith was finally able to leave his grief-stricken sister sleeping under a sedative and in the capable hands of a trained nurse. He stepped down into the London street and turned left along the pavement towards his car. He was thinking of Joan's last words and cursing his own helplessness.

Farther up the road a newsboy was shouting, and almost automatically Smith bought a paper. The headlines screamed at him.

EIGHT MORE VICTIMS OF THE
KILLER DRUG
TOP CHEMISTS WORK DAY AND
NIGHT TO PERFECT AN ANTIDOTE

There was no need to read any further, for the headlines said everything. Smith turned away as the newsboy began to shout again.

" . . . Red Death kills five more . . . Read all about it . . . Latest football news . . . Pay snatch in Chelsea . . . Red Death kills five more . . . Red Death — "

Smith slammed the door of his car and shut the words out. Starting the engine he turned out into the street. The car began to gather speed and his thoughts moved faster to keep pace.

The tension built up in his chest again and he could still hear the echoes of the newsboy's shouts ringing in his ears. He had to stop for a traffic light and the red halt sign seemed to burn into his brain. The red light was the symbol of the red death.

The amber flashed and mercifully the red light went out. Then it was green and he was moving again. The newsboy's shouts still tormented him. His chest was constricted and Joan was sobbing helplessly *"Somebody must be able to do something!"*

Then abruptly the tension snapped. And without making any conscious decision the little man knew that for the first time in his life he had lost a battle to his conscience. He was going to ignore an order that came direct from the Prime Minister of Great Britain.

He pulled up at the next telephone booth and went inside. Deliberately he dialled a Mayfair number. The number of a flat in Rushlake Terrace, and of a man named Simon Larren.

2

Arrival in Athens

Simon Larren was a natural killer. He had been very thoroughly trained during the grim days of 1939 – 45, and his favourite allies were silence, darkness and a knife. Once he had experienced love and marriage and it had almost changed his life, but then his beloved Andrea had been murdered and it had taken him a long time to track down her killers. When the blood-stained path of death and violence came to an end there was only one place left in civilized society for a man of his kind — and that was in an organization such as the one run by the unassuming Mr. Smith.

He sat on a wooden seat as though idly watching the ducks by the Serpentine in Hyde Park. He was a tall, unsmiling man, with a strange brooding quality about his grey-green eyes. He was bare-headed and the evening breeze was stirring his dark hair. At the moment he was puzzled.

His speculations were terminated by the appearance of the short little man in the dark suit and the bowler hat. As usual Smith carried a cheap briefcase and a rolled umbrella. He was the prototype of all the insignificant, clerkish little men in the city; a nonentity who would be lost with a million duplicates in the underground or the rush hour buses. No one except Larren gave him a second glance.

Smith reached the park bench and sat down.

"Hello, Larren," he said shortly. "Thanks for coming."

The note of gratitude was out of place and Larren knew that whatever Smith wanted of him it was no ordinary job. He probed with his answer.

"I had to come, my curiosity got the better of me. I couldn't reason out why you wanted to come out here instead of calling me into the office."

Smith gave him a hard look. "My office is strictly for business — official business.

I don't invite people round there for half an hour's idle conversation." He stressed the words deliberately and for a moment his grey eyes revealed a glimpse of the man behind the façade.

Larren waited.

Smith said abruptly, "You've heard of Ameytheline — the nerve drug that was passed as perfectly safe and then found to cause delayed paralysis and ultimately death among regular takers?"

The question was merely a technicality, an opening line for what was to follow, for no one could have failed to have heard of the red death.

Larren nodded. "When the thalidomide drug was marketed and then found to cause deformed births among expectant mothers there was a public outcry. A watchdog committee was set up by the Government to ensure that from then onwards all new drugs would be properly tested by their makers before being prescribed to the public. But Ameytheline had slipped the screening before the committee was set up. The creeping paralysis was such a long-delayed reaction that at first the doctors failed to see any connection, but the vivid red rash that accompanied the closing stages provided the unexplained link which they finally traced back to the drug."

"That's right." Smith's voice was harsh. "Ameytheline was a sleep-inducing tranquillizer. It was considered so safe that it was even prescribed in rare cases for children. My five-year-old niece was one of those rare cases. She suffered from recurring nightmares and the doctor couldn't find the cause. So, he prescribed small doses of Ameytheline to help her sleep. She's sleeping now. I've just watched her die."

Again Larren waited.

Smith went on quietly. "She was just five years old, Larren. A pretty little kid — or at least she was before that red rash covered her face." His voice hardened again. "And there are going to be others, Larren. A hell of a lot more people are going to die before this is stopped."

Larren said. "Every top research chemist in the country is working to find an antidote. Maybe they'll break through."

Smith's grey eyes bored into Larren's face. For a moment he fought his inner battle a second time, and then he said softly, "There already is an antidote, Larren. The antidote for Ameytheline was discovered eight days ago."

There was a taut silence. Then Larren said flatly, "Go on."

"Ameytheline was the discovery of a brilliant young Italian chemist named Paolo Castel. At one time he worked for a large research centre in Rome, but when he perfected Ameytheline he was working privately. He had his own laboratory near Milan. When it was discovered that Ameytheline was a killer Castel did everything he could to make amends. He worked day and night to find an antidote, and finally he succeeded. He died the same day in an eighty mile per hour car crash just outside Milan."

Smith's voice was curt and factual now. "We only know that Castel had been successful because of a couple of notes he left behind. The actual formulae and his samples were missing when his home was examined. We think that Castel was probably rushing into Milan to report his success personally to the firm that marketed the drug, and in his haste he killed himself."

"Or was killed." Larren interjected softly.

Smith shook his head. "The fact that someone was close at hand to remove the antidote doesn't necessarily mean that Castel was murdered. I know it looks that way, but there are a couple of facts that don't agree. One is that although the Italian police can't rule out the possibility that Castel's car was tampered with, they have examined the wreckage thoroughly and failed to find anything to suggest sabotage. And two is that the man behind the theft of the antidote is most probably Castel's own father, and although he's an ex-racketeer and hired killer I think he'd draw the line at murdering his own son."

Smith paused to draw an angry breath for the tension was building up inside him as he talked. Larren remained silent, knowing that the little man would continue.

Smith said, "Castel's father was a man named Angelo Valedri. He was born in a remote village in the deep south of Italy in 1901, and seventeen years later he emigrated alone to the United States to look for work. He did a few wild things like robbing gas stations, beating up shopkeepers for a small time protection racket, and knifing his mistress's husband; then he finally found himself a nice steady job with good pay and short hours. The firm he worked for was called Murder Incorporated and all he had to do was a spot of corpse making now and again. The job suited him perfectly, and at nineteen he was one of the ablest killers in the organization. He was smart too. Smart enough to get out of the paid killer bracket and into the racketeering class where the big money was. He was a rich man by the time Murder Incorporated began to lose its grip, and one of the few to get away scot free without anyone being able to actually prove anything about him. The States were getting too hot for him and in 1931 he took a ship back to Italy.

"There he almost immediately married a hard-working little waitress — who must have been some woman to have had the taming effect on him that she did. She gave him two children; a daughter named Carla nine months after their wedding, and the son Paolo a few years later in 1935. She even kept him going straight for a bit but it couldn't last. Valedri was born rotten and she could only reform him until the novelty had worn off. A year after the boy was born Valedri was shot, down by the Italian police while trying to rob a bank in Verona. He lived despite a smashed thigh bone, and was sentenced to thirty years in prison.

"His wife brought up the two children for the next few years, and then she caught pneumonia and died. Carla was then placed in a convent and Paolo was sent to one of the most expensive private schools in Italy. For Valedri still had a king-sized bank account left over from his profitable stay in the U.S. and he could well afford the best of everything for them. In fact the solicitors who handled his affairs invested his money so carefully for him that it continued to grow all the time he was in prison.

"Valedri was an unusual man, he hated society and all that it stood for, yet at the same time he was determined that his son was going to have all the advantages that the society could provide. Paolo had the best education that money could buy, and he was registered at the school under his mother's maiden name of Castel to avoid anyone knowing that his father was a convict. Even the boy himself did not know his father was alive, and like everyone else he believed that the money that paid for his keep came from his mother's will.

"Valedri eventually came out of prison four years ago with a seven year remission for good behaviour. At that time Paolo Castel had just finished university and was taking up his position as a research chemist in Rome. Valedri still wanted the boy to have every chance and made no attempt to contact him. He was afraid that the stigma of a convict's son, if it once got out, would ruin all Castel's hopes for advancement."

Smith broke off and breathed heavily for a few moments. Then he began again.

"Obviously Valedri kept an interested eye on his son's progress, and he must have received some satisfaction from reading of his success in discovering Ameytheline. But I think he was probably more interested when Ameytheline proved to be a killer, especially as his son was now the best hope for providing a quick antidote. Valedri could see the possibilities in that antidote, and he was callous enough not to care how many people died while he hunted around for the highest bidder.

"However, I don't think he would have willingly jeopardized his son's career. The boy meant too much to him. I think it was more likely that he was afraid of somebody else thinking along the same lines as himself, and so he had the boy watched for his own protection. But he couldn't protect him against the sheer bad luck of a genuine accident. Whoever was watching him in Milan probably jumped to the same conclusion that you did — namely that Castel's car had been fixed. And so he ransacked the chemist's laboratory, located his notes and the antidote samples, and then packed them off to Valedri."

Smith paused again and Larren said grimly, "And now Valedri is using them to blackmail the British Government — is that it?"

Smith nodded. "That's it. We can have it at a price."

Larren said harshly, "If that's the only way why isn't it paid? The red death is killing off the population at the rate of a score per day. Surely no price is too high to stop it."

Smith said bitterly, "But the price is too high. Valedri has not only asked for the nice round sum of eighty million pounds — he also wants us to hand over Andromavitch."

Larren was puzzled. "You mean the Russian? The scientist?"

"That's right, Larren. Professor Eugene Vladomir Andromavitch, the finest scientific brain of the century. He knows more about nuclear fission than any other two men alive put together. If we lost him to the other side and they made him talk it could ultimately cost us more lives than the red death ever will. We cannot afford to hand him over at any price."

"But what does a man like Valedri want with a scientist?"

"I don't know. That's the one big hole in the jig-saw. As far as we know Valedri has shown no previous interest in politics. His hatred includes all forms of civilized society. Maybe he hopes to auction Andromavitch to the highest bidder but I can't see him really expecting to accomplish that. And besides, if it was more money he wanted, he could simply put up the cash price on the antidote. Quite frankly I just don't know what his game is. At the moment it's stalemate, and all we can do is pray that one of our research chemists can come up with a new answer to Ameytheline before anything leaks to the Press."

Larren said softly, "Can't something be done about Valedri? It must be possible to bring him out into the open somehow."

Smith's voice became more bitter than

Larren had ever heard it before. "We don't have to find him," the little man rasped. "We know exactly where he is. But I can't touch him."

Larren said. "I don't understand."

"It's quite simple. When Valedri came out of prison he was still a rich man, and as he had no desire for any social life he leased a small, useless island in the Aegean and built himself a villa. The island is called Kyros and barely covers half a square mile. It was uninhabited before Valedri arrived and I think he leased it pretty cheaply from the Greek government.

"The point is that although we are one hundred per cent certain that Valedri must have the antidote, we have no actual proof. The Andromavitch angle made it my business and I had some of my best men on the job before I was told to lay off; and their reports show that unless somebody is being fantastically brilliant in covering his tracks then Valedri is the only man in the picture who is big enough and black enough to be behind it. But we can't prove it. And even if we could Valedri is still Castel's nearest living relative, and as the boy made no will he is legally entitled to claim all the boy's effects. And as Castel was working privately that includes his notes and samples. So you see, legally we have no grounds for asking the Greeks to hand Valedri over, and to land on Kyros and take him would be invading Greek soil and literally an act of war."

"But surely in the circumstances — "

"The circumstances are that even if Valedri was operating from a base inside England he would still be legally entitled to ask any price he likes for that antidote. The fact that he's miles away on the Aegean and there's another Government involved only complicates the main issue. The British Government has two choices; it can pay Valedri's price and buy the antidote from him — or it can reject his offer and wait for our research teams to equal Castel's achievement. And with Andromavitch as part of the price we can only follow the latter course."

Larren said slowly, "There must be something you've missed in regard to

Andromavitch. Valedri demanding that he be handed over just doesn't fit anywhere. Can you fill me in on his background?"

"I know it by heart. Andromavitch worked for the Russians for twenty-five years before he shook the scientific world by fleeing to the west. He brought his only daughter with him and begged political asylum for them both. He just couldn't take any more of the lack of freedom and constant surveillance to which he was subjected in Communist Russia. He was welcomed with open arms.

"His only living relative was the daughter who had escaped with him. He had lost track of his family during the war and his wife had died in childbirth. There was no one in Russia who could be used to exert pressure upon him and the security screen passed him as clean. In view of his exceptional mental capabilities he was considered a justifiable risk and allowed to continue his work for us.

"The daughter was accidentally drowned at a beach party near Athens while on a holiday in Greece and now he has

21

no one. There was a flap on over that at first because the body was never recovered and it was thought that she may have been picked up by the other side. However, if that had been the case the pressure would have been applied to Andromavitch long before now so she must have genuinely drowned. Apparently she was near-enough helplessly drunk at this party and the fools let her go swimming with them. By the time they'd missed her it was far too late. Since then Andromavitch has been a bit anti-social, but he still seems happy enough when he's working."

"And what's his reaction to Valedri's demand?"

"He hasn't been told. He hasn't really got anything to leave behind now, and in the circumstances he may be quite willing to sacrifice himself to bring the red death to an end. The Government can't trade him, but he's a somewhat gallant old man and it wouldn't be out of character for him to simply give us the slip if he could and give himself up."

"So what's the answer?"

Smith gave him a hard look. "There isn't one. We have no provable grounds for offending the Greek Government, or for touching Valedri. The official order is to leave the matter alone and wait for the chemists to save the situation."

He turned his gaze away and looked out over the darkening water of the Serpentine. It was late evening now and the sun had disappeared from the sky. Courting couples were strolling through the park. Larren watched the little man's profile again, waiting for him to go on. Smith was silent, just a pompous little clerk in a bowler hat now that Larren could no longer read his deep grey eyes.

Then very softly the little man spoke again.

"Of course, the ideal thing would be for some other criminal element to step in; some murdering blackmailer as ruthless as Valedri himself. If Valedri was eliminated and his killer offered the antidote for a price that did not include Andromavitch the Government wouldn't hesitate to pay."

He glanced back at Larren and added,

"But that's too much to hope for. Valedri has fitted Kyros out with electrified trip wires, a small team of bodyguards and patrolling dogs. Nobody could get near him."

He paused again and then quietly contradicted himself. "That is not unless he was reached through Carla. She had to leave the convent because her glands just weren't suited to a sexless life, and Valedri saw no harm in contacting her. They get on quite well and she visits him often. At the moment she's living high in Athens and staying at the Hotel Tripolis."

He smiled bitterly. "But even then only a fool would try it, and even if he succeeded he would have the Greek police to contend with. The law doesn't allow any man to be murdered without retribution — not even a death-deserving scum like Valedri."

He stood up suddenly. "There's no point in moping over something I can't do anything about," he said briskly. He picked up his umbrella and briefcase and then turned to give Larren a tight smile.

"I'm sorry if I bored you by rambling on. You'll forget it all of course, some of it comes under the heading of secret information." The smile hardened and died and he added, "That's a direct order, Larren."

Larren said nothing.

Smith straightened his jacket and then said as an after-thought, "By the way, what I really wanted to see you about was to tell you that you have some leave due. I'm sorry I took so long in getting round to it."

He said goodbye and walked briskly away along the lake-side.

★ ★ ★

Eighteen hours later a B.E.A. jet airliner landed at Athens airport and Simon Larren was one of the last passengers to descend the gangway. He thanked the smiling stewardess and in answer to her respectful farewell he assured her that he would most certainly enjoy his holiday stay in Greece and the surrounding islands.

3

Carla Valedri

Larren took a taxi from the airport and booked a cheap room at the Hotel Sparta. He had checked the hotel list at the airport to find another hotel in the same street as the Hotel Tripolis, and he was well satisfied to find that he could observe the main entrance to the more expensive hotel from his window. He went out immediately and hired himself a car, a small green Renault saloon which he parked outside the hotel in readiness, and then he returned to his room and settled down to wait. He knew that Carla Valedri resided in the hotel on the opposite side of the street, and if he waited long enough then she must eventually pass either in or out. It was just a matter of patience.

He had a meal sent up while he waited, and as he ate he took a postcard-sized photograph from his pocket and studied it thoughtfully.

The picture had obviously been taken at a night club table and the central figure was one of that small percentage of women who could literally be classed as voluptuous. There was a man seated on either side of her but they were no more than part of the background; the woman dominated the whole table. She wore a black evening gown that ended just above the line of her nipples and even in the photograph her bearing was of shameless pride. Her mouth was full and smiling, her eyes were bold, and her hair was a falling sea of raven-black waves. She was undoubtedly a wanton.

The photograph had arrived through the post at Larren's flat in Rushlake Terrace a few hours before he had left for London Airport that morning. There had been no accompanying letter, but Larren knew instinctively that this was the last piece of assistance that Smith could give him. He had Carla Valedri's photograph and now he was on his own.

As he studied the picture he suddenly

realized that there were going to be some awkward complications if Carla Valedri didn't speak English, for he spoke no Greek. He knew that normally Smith would never have selected a man with no knowledge of the language, but this was no normal job and there had been no question of selection. An agent with a killer streak and a preference for working completely alone was a rarity even in Smith's organization, and there were even fewer men who could have accepted the unorthodox approach that the little man had used, or the grim terms that he had been forced to dictate. Smith's last warning to forget their conversation had been a pointed warning that Larren was absolutely alone.

The hours passed slowly as Larren maintained his patient vigil. He rang down for a bottle of scotch and a soda syphon and drank sparingly as the dusk thickened into darkness and the night life of Athens gathered speed. Even here, away from the crowded centres of Omonia and Syntagma Squares the pulse of the city was beginning to beat.

Then at last the waiting ended. A sleek red sports car pulled up with a squeal of brakes outside the Hotel Tripolis, and Larren sat up slowly as his gaze rested on the raven-haired woman who was smiling and laughing beside the driver. Carla Valedri's nature and bearing stamped her clearly, even at this distance.

Her escort looked everything that the driver of a fast, open-topped sports car should be. He was young and handsome, his dark hair sleekly oiled and his teeth very white in his sun-bronzed face. He wore an open-necked white shirt and a slim gold chain hung about his throat. He was not one of the two men from the night club photograph.

Carla Valedri pushed open the door of the car and her lips moved in words that Larren couldn't read. Then she turned and hurried into the hotel. The young Greek settled back in his seat and made no move to drive away.

Larren frowned. He might have expected competition with a bombshell like Carla, but the Greek in the sports car was going to prove a formidable rival. Then he realized abruptly that as the Greek was waiting for Carla then they were obviously going out again. And having made visual contact there was nothing more that he could do by sitting up at his window like a nosey neighbour.

The photograph was no longer needed now and he swiftly ripped it into small pieces and flushed them away in the bathroom. For a moment he wondered whether he ought to take a gun, or the razor-edged sheath knife that he favoured more, but he decided against both. They would prove too incriminating if they were noticed. Briskly he descended to the street.

The red sports car was still there as he climbed into his own Renault, and he hoped earnestly that Carla would not keep her boy friend waiting for too long. He found a street map of Athens in the door pocket of the Renault and made a pretence at studying it until Carla reappeared some five minutes later.

Carla had changed into a low cut evening dress and had added a white wrap and gloves, and she was still laughing and smiling. The young Greek gave her a quick approving grin and held open the door of the sports car as she climbed in beside him. He started his engine and nosed the car slowly out into the traffic.

The red sports began to pull away and Larren quickly started his own Renault. He checked his mirror and then turned into the road to follow, and then he swore abruptly as another car a few yards ahead pulled out in front of him and forced him to brake sharply.

The car was a big American Chevrolet and Larren recalled that it had stopped beneath his window at almost the same moment that the red sports had stopped before the Hotel Tripolis. But the fact hadn't registered properly then and it didn't register now because he was concentrating on keeping the sports car in sight.

However, the Chevrolet lost no time in gathering speed, and although it was between him and his quarry Larren could still see the low red car ahead. He started to close up in order to overtake and then changed his mind. It was a mistake to follow a car by sitting right on its tail, and as the Chevrolet was maintaining the same speed it was best to let the American car remain between them.

It was not until the red sports had cut across two main traffic lanes with the Chevrolet still keeping its position that Larren realized that the second car was also trailing Carla Valedri.

The knowledge forced Larren to drop farther behind, letting the red car get out of sight but still keeping the Chevrolet in view. This was one complication that he hadn't expected and it caused his unsmiling mouth to tighten grimly. The man in the American car was broad-shouldered, thick-necked and had sparse black hair, but that was all Larren could tell from the back view. He wondered who the man was — or who he represented.

The red sports car led both its pursuers down to the seafront and turned up the wide road towards Cape Sounion that Larren had travelled in the taxi on the way from the airport. The breeze blew in coolly from the dark sea as they passed the beach bars and restaurants with strings of coloured lights showing up the open air tables. The driver of the sports began to demonstrate his car's abilities and soon the airport flashed by on the left-hand side. Larren had the Renault flat out and found it difficult to keep the pace.

He swore softly as the tail lights of the Chevrolet slowly pulled away ahead of him. They were out of the suburbs now and there were open stretches of beach spacing the seafront villas on their right. After passing the airport the road had shrunk from a six to a four-laned highway, but it was still a dual-carriageway and made no difference to the sports car's speed.

Then suddenly Larren found that he was closing the gap with the Chevrolet and realized that the car in front was slowing up. He touched his brake pedal gently and eased off the accelerator in order to keep his distance, and then he saw why the Chevrolet had slowed.

The red sports had stopped and was

turning up the drive to one of the sea-front villas, and the sounds of music and laughter that came from the house made it plain that there was a party of some kind going on. The Chevrolet shot past at reduced speed and a moment or two later Larren's Renault followed. Neither Carla or her driver bothered to look back.

The Chevrolet kept going for another three or four hundred yards and then that too began to stop. Without hesitation Larren pulled past it and continued to keep his foot down as he roared on into the night. Half a mile farther on the road curved enough for him to stop without any risk of being observed and he pulled the Renault off the road.

He waited just in case the man in the Chevrolet was trying to be smart and came after him, but after five minutes he climbed out of the Renault and gazed back up the road. There was still no sign of the big American car.

So the man in the Chevrolet must have settled down to watch the villa. Larren wondered what the hell was going on.

Finally he decided to ignore the

complications and concentrate on what was now his main problem — how to gate-crash the party at the villa and charm Carla Valedri away from her present escort. He knew that every delay he made meant more victims for the red death, and now that he had located Carla and tracked her down this far he could not afford to waste the time already spent.

For over an hour he stood by his car or paced around it, wrestling with a dozen different ideas. He evolved plans, discarded them, searched for new ones and rejected them again. Finally he decided that he could think better while driving and climbed back into the Renault.

The road became a two lane switchback that curved and dipped along the magnificent stretch of coastline known as the Atki Apollon. Even by starlight the endless string of wide bays and tiny coves was beautiful, but Larren barely noticed. Then abruptly a pair of dazzling headlights swept round a bend towards him, the car behind them slithering drunkenly across the road.

Larren was blinded. He stood hard on the brake and fought the Renault to a screaming, slithering stop. Although he couldn't see instinct told him that the car coming at him was in the middle of the road. He ran up the sandy verge out of its way and heard it shoot past him. Then the Renault was at a standstill and he opened his eyes. He was sweating hard.

He cursed the drunken driver who had missed him so narrowly and then broke off abruptly. He almost forgave the man who had nearly killed him as he realized that here was one idea for literally gate-crashing the party at the villa.

He thought no more about the incident as he reversed the Renault and raced back the way he had come. He stopped at the first bar he came to and purchased six bottles of wine and two of spirits and then drove on again.

He slowed down as he neared the villa and slipped his shoulders into the safety straps that were fitted to the car. He spotted the parked Chevrolet still waiting on the other side of the road and decided that he might as well make a good impression with all concerned. He allowed the Renault to wander over the road in the same manner as the car that had almost ran him into the sea.

The driver of the Chevrolet didn't even look up. He had switched on his interior light and settled down for a long wait with a book.

Larren shrugged and aimed the bonnet of the Renault at the far side gatepost that flanked the drive of the villa where the red sports car had vanished.

At the last moment he swung his legs up on to the passenger seat beside him. Twisting his body in the straps he threw his left arm over the back of the seat and hung on with his face pressed against the upholstery as the car crashed.

The sound almost deafened him as the Renault's bonnet shrieked and buckled. The force of the impact jerked fiercely at his shoulders but the safety straps held him as the car skidded round in a half circle and finished up by blocking the gateway. There was a brief moment of silence as the echoes of the collision died away and then there was a uproar of startled cries from the villa.

Larren unbuckled the straps and climbed out slowly to inspect the damage. He had buckled the front of his car far more than he had intended to, but at least it was nowhere near as bad as he had feared from that hideous shrieking sound. The concrete gatepost had been faced with yellow plaster and a lot of that had cracked and shaken off, but on the whole there was no real harm done.

He turned to face the small crowd that came running down the drive towards him. Shocked for a moment into sobriety their faces showed relief when they saw him standing unharmed beside the car. A barrage of questions flew at him in meaningless Greek.

He took a deliberately unsteady pace towards them and made his voice sound slightly slurred and shaken as he answered in English. "I — I'm terribly sorry. My car skidded and I ran into your gatepost."

Another wave of words he couldn't understand and then a short, barrel-chested man with excited hands pushed forward from the crowd. "You speak English?" he asked.

Larren nodded. "Yes, I am English. Look, I'm terribly sorry about this. You must let me pay for the damage."

The crowd had spread out to examine the gatepost and the car and were grinning at him widely. They had obviously been a merry crowd before the disturbance and now that they were realizing that nobody was hurt the sobering effect was vanishing. Only the little man with the gesturing hands still seemed anxious.

"You are not . . . not hurt?" He asked, groping for words.

Larren patted himself reassuringly and gave a shaky smile. "No. It's all right. I'm not hurt." He put his hand in his inside pocket and pulled out his wallet. "Please, where is the man who owns this house. I must pay him for the gate."

A second Greek with a dark moustache had appeared and waved the money away. The English-speaking one explained.

"This house is Dimitri's. The gate does not matter."

The man named Dimitri nodded and spluttered in Greek, almost forcibly he pushed Larren's hand holding the wallet back inside his pocket. The rest of the crowd gathered round, one or two of them struggling with English but most of them talking Greek. More people were coming out of the villa and many of them were women, full of feminine curiosity now that they were assured there was no blood and the men made no attempt to keep them away. Someone mentioned the police but the revellers clearly had no desire to entertain any more intruders and the lone voice was shouted down.

Larren made another attempt to get his wallet out and open it. "Please," he insisted. "It was my fault and you must let me pay. I have been drinking a little, otherwise I would not have lost control."

"Everybody drinks," a new voice laughed.

Larren tried again but there was another chorus of refusals and gestures of approval as Dimitri pushed the offer aside.

As though in desperation Larren stopped trying to get his money out and pulled open the door of the Renault instead. He picked up a bottle of wine in each hand and held them out.

"Look, you are having a party. If you will not let me pay for the gate then you must let me help to drown the memory of the interruption. There are some more bottles here you must have. It is the least I can do."

Again the clamouring voices and the refusals. The wine was waved aside but there was just a moment's hesitation this time.

Larren insisted that they allow him to get the party back in swing by accepting the bottles. Then somebody made a suggestion that seemed to delight them all. The little man who spoke English laughed and clapped Larren on the shoulder.

"Sir, we will drink your wine with one . . . one . . . how you say? . . . one condition." He seemed to swell with pride as he got the word out. "You must join our party and help us to drink it."

41

It was Larren's turn to hesitate and refuse.

"No," he exclaimed. "I couldn't intrude like that. I just want to make up for spoiling your party."

"But we insist. You must join us. You must not drive the car until you have rested."

The grinning, laughing faces surged around him and Larren knew that even if he were serious in refusing he would have difficulty in backing out now. His refusals grew weaker and finally he gave way with well-feigned embarrassment.

Willing hands helped to lift the remaining bottles of wine and spirits out of the car and then some of the younger men set to work to straighten the vehicle up and park it off the driveway. They wouldn't even let him help with that.

Finally he was swept along with the crowd as they returned to the villa. Someone pushed a full glass in his hand and he was pleasantly surprised to find that it was scotch and soda. His gate-crashing attempt had been a complete success.

4

Wild Party

The barrel-chested little man who spoke English was named Georges. He introduced himself and a stream of other curious but friendly people who crowded round to pump Larren's hand and slap him on the shoulders. Everyone seemed delighted with the small amount of excitement his abrupt appearance had provided, and the whole thing was treated as a great joke. They all called him Simon the moment he revealed his name and kept up a noisy chatter of questions about where did he come from and where was he going. They were all flushed with liquor and somebody spoiled his scotch by topping it up to the brim with bitter retzina wine.

He was unable to discover what the celebration was all about, but the expensive gowns of the women, the lush

43

fittings of the villa, and the abandoned way in which the whole party were pairing off into amorous couples and drinking themselves silly helped to tell him that they were part of the smart young night club set. There were well over a score of people there with both sexes evenly represented, and the fact that stocks had been getting low when he offered his contribution of eight additional bottles of wine and spirits made him their hero of the hour. He intended to explain that he had been laying in a stock for a party of his own later but the opportunity never arose and the lie was not needed.

The novelty of a strange Englishman in their midst eventually began to wear off and the party gave way to other interests. However, Dimitri, who either owned or rented the villa, was still just sober enough to remember that he was supposed to be host. He pulled Larren away from the shrinking group who had somehow groped their way back to stage one of the conversations and were again asking vague questions about was he English and did he come from London, and led him over to the corner of the room.

Here he was introduced to a second Georges, a thin anaemic young man who was barely capable of holding his wine glass steady, and a well-proportioned, giggling girl in her twenties who was struggling to hold him upright. The girl had coy brown eyes and chestnut curls and her name was Nina. Dimitri added the information, "Nina speak English," and then he took over the job of supporting the young man and led him staggering away through a door that apparently led to the back of the house.

Larren was left alone with Nina. She pushed closer to him, gazing up at his face with her wide brown eyes and asking the same silly question that he had already answered a score of times in the last half hour.

"Do you speak English?"

"I am English," he said wearily. And then he asked, "Where has Dimitri gone with your friend Georges?"

She giggled. "Do not worry about

Georges. Dimitri will push him out into the fresh air and he will be sick. Then he will fall down somewhere and go to sleep."

She became aware that he had no glass, for he had placed his ruined scotch on the mantelpiece and simply left it there, and immediately she insisted that they had another drink. She swallowed her own wine in one gulp and put her arm around his waist as she led him back across the room to the table where the drinks were. The acting barman was slumped unconscious against the nearest wall and they helped themselves. Larren poured Nina another glass of the sweet red wine she was drinking and mixed a treble scotch and soda for himself. He reasoned that he had paid for it, and at this stage he damned well needed it.

Nina drank the glass of wine the way an Irish labourer would sink a pint of bitter, and while she was momentarily occupied Larren searched the room for Carla Valedri and her escort. He had noted that the red sports car was still parked in the driveway as he came in, but so far he had seen no sign of his quarry. Before he could think too much on the subject Nina fell against him and he was forced to concentrate on holding her up.

After a moment she recovered and looked up at him, tossing her head back to throw the chestnut curls out of her eyes. "I like you, Simon," she said, and even managed to sound serious for a moment. Then she linked her hands round the back of his neck and repeated the words with a giggle. At the same time she wriggled her body against him just to remind him what sort of a party this was.

The first Georges, the one who spoke English, came stumbling past with the wine in his glass spilling over the carpet. He grinned at Larren and closed one eye in a dirty wink as the other eye ranged over Nina's clinging form. "Is a good party — yes?" He shouted. And then moved on without waiting for an answer.

Larren took a good, steadying drink at his king-sized scotch and then tried to steer the girl over to the nearest couch. Before he could reach it another couple dropped down into its depths and went straight into a passionate embrace. Larren looked round the whole room but every armchair was already occupied. Then somebody switched on a record player and a jazz band roared at full blast into the room. Nina immediately wanted to dance.

Larren held her up while she made a clumsy attempt to jive. One or two other couples followed her example but the music was far too fast for their sluggish limbs and it was switched off as fast as it came on. Nina looked thoroughly disappointed but she smiled again when a slow waltz replaced it. She leaned up to Larren and nuzzled his ear as the other couples moved clumsily around them.

It was now over an hour since Larren had entered the villa and he was beginning to think that he had made a mess of his car for nothing. And then over Nina's head he saw Carla Valedri come into the room through the door where Dimitri had steered Nina's previous escort.

She was wearing a glittering dress of blue-black silk, a colour obviously chosen so that the low cut neckline could emphasize the creamy texture of her full breasts. She was smiling and her eyes sparkled as she looked over her shoulder at the man behind her. He was the young driver of the sports car and the livid bite mark on the side of his throat made it clear why they had not rushed out to the car crash, or put in an appearance since.

Larren watched them cross over to the table where the drinks were and then turned his attention back to Nina before his interest could be noticed. He remembered the other couples he had seen drifting through that door and told himself he should have guessed that it led to the bedrooms. There was a limit to how far you could go in an armchair surrounded by dancers, even among this crowd.

He felt Nina's arms pulling hard at his shoulders to bring his head down and was unable to avoid her seeking lips. She tried to excite him by movements of her tongue and little squirms with her body. Then she let her head fall back and said huskily, "I like you, Simon. You're nice. You want to — to — " She had to stop there helplessly because she didn't quite know how to express it in English. Her expression was petulant and stupid and Larren wondered how the hell he was going to get rid of her.

She was annoyed with him suddenly. She stepped back and said sharply, "I want another drink."

Larren took her arm and led her back to the table with its scattered bottles. The way she staggered suggested the obvious way to get rid of her and he kissed her to keep her happy again before propping her up against the wall.

He found two half pint glasses and filled them a quarter full with neat scotch, then he added a quarter of gin, a quarter of black rum, and topped the lot up with vodka. He dropped a cocktail cherry and a slice of orange peel in each and turned towards her. Nobody was taking any notice of them as he handed her one of the glasses.

"That's what we call a Piccadilly Power Punch," he said. "And if you can drink it you're as good as anybody here."

Nina looked at it doubtfully and then giggled.

"Together now," Larren coaxed. "One . . . two . . . three!"

He tilted the glass to his lips and took two big swallows as Nina did likewise. The girl screwed up her eyes as the burning mixture hit her throat and Larren promptly lowered the rest of his glass and tipped three parts of it into a nearby ice bucket.

Nina got half of her drink down before she had to break off into a fit of spluttering. She gaped at Larren through tear-stained eyes and he felt genuinely sorry for her as he calmly drained what was left in his glass. With a gallant effort Nina closed her eyes again and gulped at the wicked mixture in her hand. She finished it and all but collapsed.

Larren steered her gently across the room and through the door where all the other couples kept vanishing. He was in another spacious, comfortably furnished room, but he could see a bed through the door on his left. There were more couples reclining here for part of the party had overflowed, but Larren propelled Nina towards the bedroom and ignored them.

Nina's face was white and sweating and her knees sagged as they entered the bedroom. Larren caught her as she fell and laid her gently on the rumpled bed. She was out cold and he knew she was going to be cruelly sick when she came round. He eased his conscience by trying to picture her white face with the ugly symptoms of the red death, and telling himself that it was better that she should be sick than that others should die. Then he left her and went back to the party.

He mixed himself another drink, mostly soda this time, and then looked round for Carla Valedri. He spotted her almost instantly on the other side of the room; her escort was relaxing in a large armchair and Carla was sitting on the arm beside him. Next to them was a table supporting the record player and a stack of records, and he decided that that was a good enough excuse to move one stage nearer. Calmly he strolled across the room and began to thumb through the record albums.

The party was much quieter now, for many of the guests had either passed out or vanished with their partners into the villa grounds or the extra bedrooms upstairs. Larren heard Carla talking to her companion in Greek just behind him and wondered again what he would do if she didn't speak English. If she did then that in itself would be sufficient excuse for him to start talking to her; but if she didn't then his night's work would have been in vain.

He was still wondering how he could best create an excuse to speak to her when a lone reveller stumbled through the doorway to provide the perfect answer. He took two steps across the thick carpet, tripped and nose-dived smack into the table where Larren was standing. He re-bounded helplessly and fell against Larren's legs, bringing the tall English man down on his back and sending the contents of his glass over Carla Valedri's stockinged leg.

The drunk was already snoring in a deep sleep as Larren pulled himself up. Carla Valedri was laughing and the young Greek with her was smiling broadly. Larren forced a grin on to his face and apologized.

"I'm sorry about that. The damned fool caught me by surprise."

He waited tensely for her answer and it seemed an unnecessarily long time before she replied in perfect English. "It does not matter. You are not hurt — and he will sleep it off."

Larren concealed his relief over the fact that his biggest obstacle had not materialized. "But your stockings," he said ruefully, gesturing to where the whisky and soda still trickled down her trim calf.

He drew a handkerchief from his pocket and knelt before her. He almost took hold of her foot but at the last moment he hesitated and held the handkerchief out to her instead.

She smiled sweetly. "Go ahead."

Larren answered the smile and then firmly gripped her ankle and got on with the job. He rubbed the spilt liquor dry deftly and without embarrassment because he sensed that that was the way she would enjoy it. Her escort's smile dissolved abruptly into a hard look but Larren ignored that. His job was to charm Carla — not the boy friend.

When he stood up she studied him curiously. "Are you English or American?" she inquired at last.

The old question, thought Larren, but at least it was phrased more intelligently. "English," he said.

She smiled. "I thought I knew everyone who came to Dimitri's parties, but I'm afraid I don't know you."

Larren explained how he had crashed into the gatepost.

She laughed. "We saw that from the upstairs window, but we didn't come down." She darted a teasing look at the young Greek beside her. "We were busy at the time."

Larren smiled broadly. There was no point in pretending not to notice the remark, for despite her cool, polite tone she was still a wanton and did not particularly care who knew it.

She looked back at him and said calmly, "My name is Carla, and this is Savino. Who are you?"

Christian names were obviously sufficient so Larren simply said, "Simon."

Carla gave him a seductive look. "Hello, Simon."

The man named Savino merely nodded shortly. His eyes told Larren to clear off.

Larren continued to smile at Carla. He smiled rarely, but when he did it was usually for a woman, and they usually responded. He knew that for the moment Carla was interested.

"Does Savino speak English?" he asked, partly because it would be useful to know and partly because it seemed the next logical step in the conversation.

The Greek answered for himself. "I speak a little," he said. His eyes were still doing most of his talking and he put one arm around Carla's waist and rested his hand upon her hip to demonstrate that she was already claimed.

Carla pushed his hand down but at the same time she turned to smile at him.

"Savino, fetch me some wine," she said sweetly.

Savino hesitated and seemed on the brink of refusing, and then he pushed himself up slowly from the armchair.

Then Carla looked back at Larren. "Simon, perhaps you would like a drink too?"

Larren knew that if he pushed this indignity on to the Greek then Savino could explode, his eyes were that ugly. But he also sensed that Carla was pushing this just for the fun of it, and if he backed away from the possibility of enraging Savino then he was finished.

He said calmly, "I'll have a whisky and soda."

He thought Savino was going to hit him but somehow the Greek kept his temper. The young man glared at him balefully for a moment and then walked over to what was left of the drinks. Larren half turned to watch him go.

Savino passed within a couple of paces

of two men who sat at a table near the door and Larren saw them give him a hard look as he passed. The nearest of the two was a gross fat man who overflowed his seat, while his companion was a dark-faced man in glasses. Larren had noticed them a couple of times during the evening as they swirled around in the crowd, but now the pace had died and they sat alone over a pack of cards and a wine bottle. He wondered what Savino had done to displease them.

He became suddenly aware that Carla had risen to her feet and turned back to face her. Her eyes were afire beneath glistening lashes and she said quite bluntly, "I am getting tired of Savino, he is too possessive and becoming a bore." Her red mouth moulded into a wicked smile. "Are you possessive, Simon? or a bore?"

Larren was saved from having to answer by the abrupt arrival of Savino returning with the drinks.

For the next half hour Carla kept the conversation at mild flirtation level and seemed to be hardly aware of Savino fuming beside them. Larren wasn't too happy with the situation as he didn't particularly want an open fight with the young Greek, but the job demanded that he back up her chatter. He had progressed beyond hope in the past few hours and it was too late to back-pedal now.

Drunken revellers still wandered in and out of the room and a small bunch had re-grouped around the drinks table, but it was clear that the party was breaking up. The record player was broken and there was very little left in the bottles. The atmosphere of cigarette and cigar smoke was becoming stifling, even though the windows were all open.

Savino was very much the worse for drink and Carla was swaying tipsily. Larren still felt clear-headed despite the few mouthfuls of the alcoholic mickey-fin he had swallowed when he had tempted the luckless Nina into knocking herself out. Slowly Larren became aware that apart from himself there were only two other people in the villa who were relatively sober; they were the two men at the card table who had glared at Savino so ferociously. They were both unobtrusively watching Carla Valedri and he sensed that like Savino they were not pleased with his intrusion. There were more complications than seemed possible surrounding this raven-haired beauty and instinct warned him to walk warily.

There was an eventual lull in Carla's talk and Larren felt obliged to fill it.

"What's happened to everybody?" He asked. "The place seems empty all of a sudden."

Carla smiled. "Some of them will be upstairs in the bedrooms, but a lot of them will be down on the beach. This villa is only a hundred yards from the sea." The memory gave her an idea for she said abruptly, "Would you like to go swimming, Simon?"

"You know that I cannot swim." Savino interrupted curtly.

Larren knew that this was Savino's cue to exit and wondered how he would take it. Calmly he said, "I'd love to go swimming, but I haven't got a costume."

Carla laughed. "Bathing costumes are

not necessary at Dimitri's parties, but as you are English I will find you one. Will you excuse us, Savino."

Savino was not willing to excuse them, Larren saw it in his eyes. He tensed for the Greek to make some move but the expression in Savino's eyes faltered slowly and died. Savino had been looking over Larren's shoulder and Larren had the strange feeling that one of the men behind him had made some calming sign. He didn't like it.

When he and Carla walked past the table where the fat man and his companion sat neither looked up. Savino made no attempt to follow them.

When they got outside there was a slight breeze blowing and starlight eased the darkness of the night. Carla took Larren's arm and led him through soft, grass-tufted sand dunes, and after a few yards they covered a slight rise and he saw the black expanse of the sea. Gentle waves rippled almost soundlessly up the beach and the night seemed very still. The only sound was some distant splashing where some of the party

61

refugees played on the sea's edge. Larren guessed that most of those who had sought the beach had wanted the privacy of some of the lonelier hollows among the dunes.

They reached a small beach hut and Carla pulled away from him and went inside. After a moment she threw out a pair of men's bathing trunks and said, "I don't know whose they are, but try them on for size."

Larren picked them up and moved round to the side of the hut, guessing that she was changing within. He slipped out of his clothes and stepped into the trunks. They fitted well and the breeze played cold on his chest as he waited for Carla. He was half expecting Savino and his friends to follow him out and cause trouble, but although he listened as he waited he heard nothing.

There was a movement in the door of the changing hut and he turned. Carla Valedri stood there in a two-piece swimming costume of red silk, it was secured by two bows, one at the hip and one under her arm, and if she had

62

bought it by the inch it would have been given away. Dark shadows played on the smooth white lines of her body and she gave Larren a teasing push and then ran laughing to the sea.

Larren sprinted after her and followed her into the low waves. The water was pleasantly warm and he struck out to catch her. She avoided him for several minutes and proved herself an excellent swimmer, then she turned back and made for the shallows.

Larren was beside her as she stood up in waist deep water and he pulled her to him. Her mouth touched his hungrily for a moment and then she pulled away. Larren knew that she wanted to play and hurled himself after her. They fell and wrestled in the salt waves and her wet limbs slipped snake-like through his fingers.

She ran up the beach, but she wanted to be caught and turned with the sea still tumbling round her knees to face him. He closed the gap between them and she clung to him and made no more attempts to pull away as she answered his demanding kiss. Her half open lips had a salty, sensuous taste that caused his glands to stand up and dance. She was no better than the drunken Nina who had disgusted him, but she aroused him in a different way. The top half of her costume had floated away on a wave as they had wrestled and now the movement of her breasts against his chest stirred his blood into lust.

He tried to lift her to carry her up the beach but she twisted violently and they both toppled over again into the shallow wavelets. Carla was underneath him and still kissing feverishly, and he became aware that somehow she had pulled the bow that had supported the bottom half of her costume and that too was floating away with the movement of the sea. They were half in the waves and half out, but her desire was so commanding that it didn't matter a damn. Her kisses were fiercer and her arms were as fast as steel bands about his shoulders.

As the waves rippled around them Larren knew why Carla had wanted him out of the villa and here on the sea's edge. He knew too why she had wanted to drop Savino and find another man for what was left of the night.

Carla Valedri was an insatiable nymphomaniac.

5

Cause for Regret

Carla was reluctant to return to the villa. She was happy and contented now and the prospect of stirring any further trouble with Savino no longer seemed to appeal to her. The party was over and she wanted to be taken home, and she suggested that they should circle round to Larren's car through the villa grounds.

Larren had no objections. He guessed that Savino was probably drinking himself into a murderous rage while he waited for them to come back, and although he had no worries about the young Greek he was not quite so happy about the fat man and his dark-faced companion. There was a connection somewhere between those three and an instinct sharpened by experience told him that the combination was dangerous.

They still lay together in the warm

waves but the breeze was becoming cold on Larren's shoulders. He stood up and helped Carla to her feet, and then led her back to the small changing hut where they had left their clothes. She found a towel and handed it to him, and again his senses pulsed as he rubbed it down the soft curves of her body. They dried and dressed and then she led him back across the dunes.

The villa rose before them, its lights still spilling from every window. There was still noise from inside but it was very subdued. Carla turned away from the villa, leading him through the sweet-smelling pines that enclosed it on either side. They circled the villa and then came out on to the gravel driveway that led up to the front porch. Savino's red sports car was still there with several others; Carla looked at it and then smiled at Larren without embarrassment as they passed. Somewhat doubtfully Larren identified his own battered Renault.

She looked at the crumpled bonnet and laughed. "Will it start?" she asked.

Larren opened the passenger door for

her to get in. "I hope so," he said. "I don't think the engine suffered any damage, it's just the body-work that's dented."

He slipped into the driving seat and silently prayed that he was right as he tried the starter. For he had a solid suspicion that Carla would sooner return to Savino with his shiny sports car than wait out in the driveway while he phoned a taxi. He felt happier when the engine purred into life, sounding completely unaffected by its rough handling, but he didn't fully relax until he was back on the road with the car still behaving as though nothing had happened.

He remembered to ask her where she wanted to be taken to before heading back to Athens and the Hotel Tripolis. He settled down to drive and almost immediately she slipped her arms tightly around his shoulders and waist and began kissing him on the mouth. He was glad that he had plenty of room on the dual carriageway, and more relieved still when she finally relaxed and snuggled her head on his shoulder. She was undoubtedly a nerve-racking playmate.

After a few minutes he noticed that he had company on the road, for the headlights of another car showed up in his rear mirror. He didn't bother to slow down and see whether or not the car stayed on his tail or passed him, he simply wondered wearily whether it was Savino's red sports or the large American Chevrolet that had formed part of the convoy out to the villa.

After five minutes he decided that it must be the Chevrolet. He could only see the lights and not the car behind them, but Savino's sports was a very low car and the headlights of his pursuer were fairly high off the road. He wondered whether the unknown man behind him had been watching to make sure who was taking Carla home when the party broke up, or whether Savino or one of his associates had warned him that she had switched escorts.

The Chevrolet followed him all the way into Athens, but when he turned around Omonia Square it was no longer there. He drove on to the Hotel Tripolis, half believing that the man in the Chevrolet had become certain of their destination and would be already parked and waiting in the same street. However, there was no sign of the big American car as he pulled up before the hotel entrance, and the fact made him more uneasy than he would have been if he had been proved right. While the enemy was behind you at least he couldn't suddenly appear from any other direction.

Carla straightened up from his shoulder and said, "Can you face another drink, Simon? Or have you had enough?"

He grinned. "I'm game enough to try."

They got out of the car and he took her arm as they went into the hotel. The clerk at the desk looked at them hesitantly and offered them a strained goodnight as they passed. When they were alone in the lift Carla's face registered annoyance.

"Damn that clerk," she said angrily. "He's got the moral judgement of an old maid."

"Forget him." Larren kissed her just to prove that it was good advice.

70

The lift stopped and they walked down a carpeted corridor. The room that Carla led him into had thick pile carpets and matching furniture in dark oak. Through an open door on the far side was a large double bed with a pale pink counterpane. Carla followed Larren's gaze through the open door and shook her head regretfully.

"Not tonight, Simon. That bore downstairs would turn me out tomorrow." She smiled and added, "I would find a less respectable hotel, but they are never anywhere near as comfortable. And as there are parties like Dimitri's most nights it isn't really necessary."

He watched her pour out two final shots of scotch and they toasted each other silently. Her eyes teased him over her glass and she sipped slowly. Finally she put the glass down empty and said:

"That's it, Simon. Kiss me goodnight."

Larren put one arm about her waist and reached up to knot his fingers in her hair, pulling her head back as his lips crushed the soft moist mouth. Her eyes were still closed when he stepped back.

"Goodnight, Carla," he said softly.

And then he turned to the door. He knew better than to beg.

As he opened it he looked back and added, "I'll call you tomorrow. If it's fine we can take another bathe."

She smiled. "I'd like that. Goodnight, Simon."

She came over and closed the door behind him.

Larren walked thoughtfully back to the lift. He knew that Carla Valedri was still interested and that he had accomplished the first part of his mission. But the next stage was to get her to take him out to the island of Kyros and at the moment he had no idea of how to tackle that. He nodded vacantly to the fretting clerk as he passed through the foyer and stepped out into the street. Still thinking he turned towards his Renault.

If he had not been thoroughly trained to keep his eyes open and one part of his mind constantly alert he would not have noticed that the rear door of his car was not properly closed. But the wartime years had sharpened his senses, and the later years of working for Smith had polished them to a fine edge. The door was barely a quarter of an inch from being fully shut, but even while deep in thought the fact registered in his mind. He knew that the door had been shut when he left the car.

He paused to carefully straighten the collar of his shirt outside his jacket, and he thought fast. He could take the initiative, but the part he was playing did not yet call for any revelation of his more deadlier talents. To Carla he had to appear as the harmless but capable lover, and until he was sure what game was being played and which characters supported which side it was best that everybody else received the same impression. He knew he had to play it dumb.

He finished straightening his collar and without any further hesitation he continued towards the Renault and climbed in behind the wheel. He heard the very faintest of movements from the seat behind him but he showed no sign.

He started the car and turned out into the street. At this hour there was no traffic and he put his foot down confidently. There was another movement behind him and it took an effort to remain natural and not turn his head. Then slowly a large, masculine hand entered his range of vision, appearing from over his shoulder and deliberately holding a vicious-looking automatic just before his eyes.

It was a stupid move. The gun should have been pressing into the back of Larren's neck and not presented where he could see it with the snout angled away from him. Larren could have grabbed the wrist then and quite safely forced it away. But he didn't. He gave the start of alarm that was obviously expected of him and allowed the Renault to swerve wildly a couple of times before pretending to regain control.

A satisfied voice behind him said something very softly in Greek.

Larren said nervously, "I don't speak Greek. But if it's money you want I'll pay."

There was a pause and then the automatic was withdrawn.

"So you're English." The voice had

an American twang now. "Well I just want to talk to you, friend. So simply follow the road signs to Korinthos and the new national road until I give some more directions."

"But I don't understand. Why — "

"Just do as you're told."

The snout of the gun jabbed Larren in a more orthodox fashion and he did as he was told. The only words the man behind him spoke after that were directions on how to get out of Athens until they struck the fast new road that led to Korinthos some fifty miles away.

Larren was pretty certain that his uninvited passenger was the driver of the Chevrolet that had paid so much attention to Carla Valedri, and he wondered exactly what the man wanted. He had puzzled over that all night, and now it looked as though he was about to find out.

Soon they were driving parallel to the sea again, only now they were heading north instead of south. Several brightly lit freighters lay at anchor in the bay and beyond them lay the black outline of the island of Salamis. The road was fast with a smooth tarmac surface, and a string of bright neon signs advertising camping sites lay between them and the sea.

They reached the road signs for Elfesis and Thebes and here Larren was ordered to turn inland. Olive groves flanked either side of the road now, their gnarled trunks springing up into the headlights like the withered ranks of a separated army. The road was rougher but another order allowed Larren to slow down. A third command forced him to turn up a pitted track of red earth and twisted roots that seemed to lead to nowhere beneath the scraping branches of the olives. Then he was told to stop.

Larren switched off the engine, but he left the headlights still picking out the silver green of the olive branches, the weirdly contorted shapes of the tree trunks, and the bare, harsh earth between. Slowly he turned to take his first look at the man who had forced him out here.

The stranger was sitting well back in the rear seat, his face hidden by shadows and darkness but the gun still prominent in his hand. Larren couldn't pick out his features but he knew from the bull neck and the broad shoulders that he had not been wrong in believing that he was the driver of the Chevrolet.

The stranger smiled at him. "What's your interest in Carla Valedri?" he demanded.

Larren said vaguely, "Well she's — she's — she's a nice girl." He pretended blustering anger and added, "What does it matter to you anyway? Who are you? What do you want?"

"I want to do you a favour, friend. I want to tell you that Carla isn't a nice girl after all. You'd do much better to leave her alone. After all, if you must have a dirty night out now and again you can pick up another partner in any of the night clubs off Syntagma Square."

Larren said snappily, "I think I'm the best judge of that."

The man from the Chevrolet shook his head sadly. "You just don't seem to understand, friend. Perhaps we'd better get out of the car and I'll make the position clear."

Larren hesitated and allowed him to make a threatening gesture with the automatic before slowly opening the car door and climbing out.

The other man followed him and for a moment they faced each other beside the car. The olive grove made soft rustling noises around them, but apart from that the night was still. The man from the Chevrolet was almost as tall as Larren but his massive shoulders made him much heavier. He smiled confidently and put the automatic into his pocket.

"The fact is," he confided amiably, "that I am employed by Carla's daddy. And he doesn't want anybody interfering with little Carla until a certain business proposition he's handling is safely over. So, my job is to look after her. And you are getting in the way of my job."

Larren tried to look puzzled. "Carla didn't tell me anything about this."

The man from the Chevrolet shrugged his ox-like shoulders. "Carla doesn't know. Her daddy doesn't want to spoil her fun as long as she sticks to her regular boy friends. But new boy friends are definitely out."

"But — "

Larren never finished as the man attacked him with sudden and unexpected ferocity. A crippling blow in the stomach slammed his back against the Renault and he gasped for air as the man held him there. Another rain of sickening blows smashed about his face and chest and then a pile-driver on the side of his neck sent him slithering across the Renault's crumpled bonnet.

He hit the dry red earth and lay there choking. He heard Carla's self-acclaimed bodyguard moving round the car towards him and knew that there was more coming. And he had to take it. If he wanted to allay the man's suspicions and hope to stay near Carla, then he had to take it.

The man from the Chevrolet hauled him to his feet and propped him against the car again. He was grinning viciously and looked formidable and ugly in the shadowed light.

"Did that help to explain, friend?" he inquired. "Carla's daddy just doesn't want her messing around with strangers."

Larren said weakly, "But I don't know anything about his business. I don't want to know. I — "

He was prepared this time and twisted away to avoid the full onslaught of the next attack. He covered himself well but still he took a pounding, fighting back only clumsily and resisting the burning urge to really retaliate. When he slumped back against the car again he was aching all over and there was blood running down above his eye and out of the corner of his mouth. He could feel the warm trickle moving softly down his face.

The man from the Chevrolet was panting hard. "I don't want to have to kill you, friend," he grated. "But I'm going to settle for the next best thing. After I've finished with you you won't be able to interest Carla anyway."

Larren sensed it coming and twisted desperately. The man had lashed out with his foot with the speed and skill of a professional soccer player and the driving impact of his steel-capped boot caught Larren squarely on the front of his

80

hip bone. He had avoided being ruptured but the searing pain paralysed the whole left hand side of his body and ripped a scream of agony from his throat.

The man from the Chevrolet poised for another kick, but Larren was past taking it now. The Englishman was blinded by rage and tears, and even when half crippled he was still a killer. He thrust himself away from the car with a strength born of white hot fury, and the out-thrust index and third fingers of his left hand gouged savagely into his assailant's eyes. It was the other man's turn to scream but he was never allowed to finish. Larren's hand flashed back and then snapped forward again in an open-handed killer blow that struck the bull neck with terrible force.

The man from the Chevrolet seemed to balance drunkenly on his feet, his eyes bulging and his head lolling stupidly to one side. Then he toppled over into a sprawling heap.

Larren hung on to the door handle of the Renault and gritted his teeth until the excruciating pain in his left hip began to fade. It took a long time and the agony made him sweat.

At last he was able to let go and turn his back to lean weakly against the car. He could feel the drying blood around his eye and mouth when he moved the muscles of his face, and he groped for a handkerchief to dab it away. Then he looked down at the untidy body at his feet with its broken neck and swore angrily.

When the bodyguard didn't make his usual report it was obvious that Angelo Valedri was going to become worried about his daughter, and doubly wary of any new friends she might have made. Killing him was a mistake.

Still cursing his lack of control Larren slid shakily behind the wheel of the Renault and began to back it out of the olive grove. His hip was still on fire but at least he could drive.

6

The Empty Bed

The drive back into Athens was the most painful half hour of motoring that Larren had ever experienced. Stabs of pain pulsed through his right hip every time he thrust the weight of his leg down to depress the clutch pedal and waves of giddiness swept over him in a sickly haze. He had to grit his teeth tightly and drove very slowly. He was hardly aware of what he was doing or where he was going and simply followed an instinctive urge to get away from the olive grove and the corpse of Valedri's hired thug.

It was not until he was approaching the city that his mind began to clear, and the first landmark that he consciously recognized was the brightly-lit, Byzantine-styled monastery at Daphne. He recalled seeing it on his way out and he realized that he was no more than four or five miles from the city centre. A few moments later the Renault pulled over the crest of a long gradual hill and below lay the lights of Athens with the floodlit Acropolis rising like a ghostly island of columned ruins from a sea of stars. Larren blinked at the scene, and then abruptly decided that it was time he started thinking again. And as he was still not capable of both thinking and driving at the same time he slowed down, pulled the Renault to the side of the road, and stopped.

He caught a glimpse of his face in his rear-view mirror and realized that the first thing he had to think about was the small matter of cleaning himself up before returning to his hotel. As they were at present his bruised and bloodied features would attract far too much attention. He pulled his handkerchief from his pocket and this time rubbed hard instead of dabbing at the dried blood.

He managed to remove all the stains from the side of his mouth, and saw upon closer inspection that there was only a small split on the corner of his lip that was barely noticeable. The only real mark that he could not remove was the colouring bruise and the shallow gash above his left eye. That was going to need sticking plaster. Mercifully the pain in his hip was fading into a nagging ache, but he knew without examining it properly that there would be another multi-coloured bruise covering the whole area. He swore sourly to himself and then closed his eyes and tried to relax for a few moments.

He knew that it was important that he should think matters out and with an effort he cleared his brain, forcing the remaining after effects of his beating deep into the back of his mind. The events of the night had moved exceptionally fast and a few hours ago he had been blessing the good fortune that had put him so close to Carla Valedri. Now he could only curse the one moment of blind fury that had driven him to killing her bodyguard and could well undo all the progress he had made. He did not for a moment doubt the man's story that he had been hired by Valedri, for it was the sort of obvious precaution that a man like

Valedri would be expected to make. And the moment that Valedri learned of his man's death then any new boy friend of Carla's would automatically become suspect.

Larren realized that it would be practically useless now for him to continue his attempt to reach Valedri through Carla, and the bitter wave of frustration that swept through him completely drowned the aches of his body. If he could not persuade Carla to take him out to Kyros then what other method was there of approaching the fortified island and completing his mission? And if he failed to complete the job how many people would die from the scourge of the red death in the weeks or months that it would take for the research team of British chemists to duplicate the antidote?

He pictured again the grim features of Smith as the little man had told the story of his niece's death, and he knew that whatever he did he must not admit failure. Even without Carla there must be a way. He began recalling the events of the night yet again, going through them stage by stage and searching for a clue that would lead him to some new line of approach. The only outstanding point that he could think of that might be relevant to the case was the strange attitude of the man named Savino, and the other two men whom Larren was sure were acquainted with the young Greek.

Larren sat up suddenly, clamping his hands on the steering wheel and thinking fast. The thoughts that had been swirling vaguely through his brain for the last few minutes had abruptly merged into solid shape. Valedri's concern for his daughter and Savino's restrained fury when Larren had taken her away from the party all began to add up. Savino's fury had not been merely that of a scorned lover, if it had been that then it would have bubbled over into the open violence that Larren had expected at the party. Savino's anger at Larren's intrusion had not been wholly emotional, it was as if there was something colder and more calculating behind his desires on Carla than merely another night in bed. And the watching fat man and his companion had been there to back them up. Could their aim have been to kidnap Carla Valedri and force her father's hand?

Larren realized that it was possible. Carla was the weak link in Valedri's defences; Smith had recognized that; Valedri had seen it too: nobody who had appreciated the monetary value of the Ameytheline antidote could have missed it. It was quite possible that the party had been arranged and Carla invited solely so that Savino could spirit her away once the other guests had departed and she was drunk and helpless. And the other two men could have been sent along just in case he needed help.

Larren turned the idea over in his mind and felt sure that he was on the right track, and then another thought burst among the rest. Anyone wishing to cash in on the antidote would have to work fast before the British chemists could come up with something of their own. And although that might take months it could just as easily be a matter of days. Speed was essential. And now he had killed the man from the Chevrolet Carla had no bodyguard to watch over her.

Quite instinctively Larren knew that Carla was in danger, and almost automatically he started the car up again and headed back into Athens. The more he thought about the matter the stronger became the feeling that he was right. He drove faster, and although his hip still ached he barely noticed it.

It seemed a long time before he was again pulling up outside the Hotel Tripolis, even though the streets had been almost clear of traffic and the drive had only taken a few minutes. He stopped the car and got out, gasping as his weight fell upon his left leg and grabbing at the open door for support. He looked up at the darkened windows of the hotel and then limped slowly over to the wide glass doors. The foyer was still brightly lit and the same clerk was dozing at the desk. Larren limped past without waking him.

He took the lift up to the second floor and then moved slowly down the corridor to Carla's room. He paused outside her door, listening, and wishing that he was armed. Then he carefully tried the door handle.

The door was not locked. Larren moved through it, his palms sweating in the brief moment that he was outlined clearly in the opening. He moved to one side, pulled the door shut behind him and listened again. After a few moments he wiped his palms down his thighs to remove the sweat and switched on the light. There was no sound of sleep-heavy breathing and he already knew that the room was empty.

He crossed the few paces to the open door of the bedroom and switched the light on in there also. The bed was empty, the white sheets and the pink counterpane were thrown back and trailing on the floor. Carla's black evening dress lay across a chair back, and on the carpet beside it lay her stockings, brassière and a pair of very brief black lace panties. Larren realized that even if Carla had changed her dress to go out she would not, at this time of night, have changed her undies. She had left her bed, but not willingly. For shameless as she was, not even Carla Valedri would willingly stroll out of her hotel after midnight in the nude.

Quietly Larren switched off the lights and left the room, gently closing the door behind him. He took the lift back to the ground floor and was again careful not to wake the sleeping clerk as he re-crossed the foyer. He left the hotel and climbed back into his car. There was a hard glitter in his grey-green eyes and just the faintest trace of satisfaction around his unsmiling mouth. He was certain that Savino and his friends must be responsible for Carla's disappearance, and he was only now beginning to realize how this new twist of fate could be twisted even farther to his favour. If he could only get her out of their hands then he would have made his biggest possible step to winning her confidence, and now that Savino had shown his hand it should only need a subtle hint to convince Valedri that the Greek had also been responsible for the death in the olive grove.

Larren started the Renault and swung its bonnet away from the kerb. He knew that the most likely place to get a lead on Carla's present whereabouts was the beach villa where they had first met. There was a strong chance that Savino had taken her back there, but even if he hadn't then the man named Dimitri who owned the house would probably know where she had been taken. Larren was convinced now that the party had been a trap to get Carla out of Athens where she could be more easily smuggled away once she had drunk herself senseless, and as Dimitri owned the villa then he had to be a party to the plot.

Larren was tempted to stop at his own hotel and collect his automatic and his favourite sheath knife, but he knew he could not afford the delay. He drove straight past and then gathered speed. Soon he was back on the great six-laned highway to Sounion with the Renault touching 75 m.p.h. It was slow compared to his own MG sports, but the small saloon had not been built for speed and it was straining badly. Larren was in no mood to ease her groaning and kept his foot hard down.

He stopped when he was still a quarter of a mile from the villa, concealing the car beneath some pines on the roadside and continuing on foot. The night air had turned cold and his left leg began to play up again as soon as he began walking. He tried to convince himself that the stiffness would wear off in time and kept going.

He covered half the remaining distance to the villa before leaving the road and turning his steps towards the sea. He passed through a small strip of the sweet-smelling pines and then crossed the low sand dunes until he reached the gently breaking line of the black waves. His movements were soundless on the soft sand as he changed direction again to follow the beach down to the villa. He moved as though he was a normal part of the dark moonless night.

His leg still dragged a little but apart from that Larren felt fit and, strangely enough, almost happy. The night was an old friend, and so was the stimulating feeling of being back in a silent no-man's-land and stealthily approaching the enemy lines. His eyes were fully accustomed to the darkness now and when he neared the villa he was able to pick out its black shape against the dark sky. He exercised more caution, sinking down low and delicately maintaining his balance with his fingertips as he moved forward. The villa was in total darkness but Larren was unarmed and dealing with dangerous men — he was taking no chances. He lowered his body flat to the sand and began to cover the last sixty yards on his stomach.

He passed the little beach hut where he and Carla had changed earlier on and his movements became even more snail-like as his body slithered over the sand. He was barely moving when he stopped thirty yards short of the back porch of the villa and waited. There was still no sign of life but Larren did not trust the absolute stillness. As an agent of S.O.E. he had often lain motionless for over an hour while trying to detect the whereabouts of a hidden German sentry, and some deep and sensitive instinct was warning him that the same tactics would serve him now. The house appeared deserted but there was a feeling in Larren's bones that he could not explain, a feeling born of long experience — a feeling that he was no longer alone in the night.

Five minutes passed . . . then ten . . . and still there was nothing to suggest that there was another living soul within miles — nothing except that vague feeling of not being alone. Without that Larren would have moved on, but it remained and so he waited. Another ten minutes passed. Larren stared at the darkened porch, his eyes unblinking. He saw nothing and he heard nothing but still he could not bring himself to go on. Five more slow, crawling minutes, and then Larren gradually became aware that all his senses were concentrated on one black corner of the porch.

There had been no sound or movement to indicate that there was a man standing there, but Larren knew that his instinct had not failed him. Whoever was keeping watch was no amateur. He was a trained professional and probably a killer. Probably too he had war-time experience in enemy territory. Quite abruptly Larren knew that the unknown, unseen sentry in the darkness was a man of his own kind — and he shivered.

Larren knew that even with the skill he had gained in knifing German sentries during the war he could never get close enough to take that mystery man by surprise, and gingerly he began to back away. His palms were sweating and it took him a long while to retreat far enough to feel safe. He was cursing himself now for not having stopped for the few seconds it would have taken him to pick up his gun.

He began to think hard and realized that if it was necessary to post a sentry on the back porch then obviously there was something inside the villa that needed guarding. Equally obviously that something could only be Carla, and the danger they would be expecting would probably be the man from the Chevrolet whom Larren had already killed. Grimly Larren began to circle round to the front of the villa. The front entrance would be guarded too of course, but he had to get in somehow and it was unlikely that the second guard could be anywhere near as dangerous as the first.

Larren was able to move fairly swiftly through the dark pines which flanked the walls of the building, but slipped down on to his stomach as he came in sight of the front porch. Again he lay motionless, but after thirty seconds a faint smile stirred on his lips. As he had expected there was another sentry, but this one was no professional. The slight slap as he swatted a fly from his face had marked the man as clearly as a luminous stripe down his back.

The man was leaning deep in the shadows of the porch, but although he was invisible in the blackness it made no difference now that Larren had spotted his position. Silently Larren wriggled over to the wall of the villa on his elbows and hips. His left hip was throbbing hotly but he spared no thought for that now. He rose slowly and silently to his feet and gently smoothed his palms down his thighs to remove the sweat. Barely stirring the air he moved along the wall of the building towards the porch.

The porch was a flimsy trellis affair, and when Larren reached it he could hear his quarry breathing softly on the other side. Larren held his own breath and softly tossed a pebble he had picked up as he wormed along the ground into a clump of bushes a few yards away. It was an old trick, but this man was no expert and Larren knew that it would do. He heard the man start and move nervously on the porch. Still holding his breath he flicked a second pebble.

The sentry moved forward. He was a dark blur in the night as he came away from the porch and peered forward. He had an automatic pointed at the clump of bushes.

Very softly Larren said. "Pssst!"

The man's head jerked up and round and for a moment the side of his neck was perfectly exposed. Larren took one swift pace forward and swung the cutting edge of his palm in one murderous blow. The blow connected, the sentry sagged, and Larren deftly caught him.

He lowered the unconscious man to the ground and relieved him of his automatic, feeling very much more sure of himself with the weapon in his hand. He thought he had seen the glint of dark glasses as his victim had started to turn and checked by exploring the man's face with his hand. His fingertips found the shape of large thick-rimmed spectacles and he knew he had been right. He recalled that one of the two men who had been watching Savino had worn dark, heavy glasses.

He wondered how many more men there might be inside the villa. The fat companion of the unconscious man at his feet would make one; Savino would be two, and Dimitri would make three. A possible three men inside the house — plus the silent professional at the back porch. The odds were high but there was no one on whom he could call for help. Larren felt his heart begin to pound and his hands begin to sweat as he delicately tried the door. It opened easily but he pushed it very slowly and slipped inside while there was still barely room to squeeze through.

Larren remembered the layout of the room and began to move forward very gingerly. The room had been in a shambles when he left and he doubted whether anyone had been sober enough to clear up, so he took great care not to stumble into an empty bottle or an overturned chair, sliding his feet forward an inch at a time. The place was in total darkness and his straining ears failed to pick up any sound. He began to wonder whether he was wrong and the house was empty, but then there would have been no need for a man on watch at both entrances and he continued to take the utmost care in moving silently.

He reached the door on the far side of the room, his free hand probing ahead of him until he found it. The door was already open and he paused in the doorway and waited. His eyes strained towards the ground floor bedroom where he had dumped the unconscious Nina and he wondered if she was still there. Then he saw the faint red glow of a cigarette end, and in the same moment heard the sighing creak of a body shifting position on the bed.

He moved his position slightly so that

he could see through the open bedroom door at another angle. Immediately he saw the point of a second cigarette. Two men were smoking silently as they waited in the darkness. Were they the only two? And was Carla with them?

Larren had to know. An inch at a time he moved closer to the door. His hand was clammy around his automatic and his heart was jumping insanely.

He could hear more movements now. A low cough, another creak from a leather-padded chair, and the sound of breathing. The two red pinpoints burned and faded as the men drew on their cigarettes. The height of the red spots and Larren's memory of the room told him that the two men were sitting down. The creak of a bed spring told him that there was someone else on the bed. Another man? or Carla, bound and helpless?

Larren pondered on his next move. Another few yards and he could reach into the bedroom to flick on the light and have everyone inside at the mercy of his gun. But that would still leave the unknown man on the back porch on the loose and Larren knew instinctively that that man was far more dangerous than all the others put together. He didn't like the idea. And if Carla was not there he would have revealed himself for nothing.

However he had to do something and quite suddenly he knew how he would do it. He would snap down the light switch, shoot the two seated men before they had a chance to recover, and then plunge the villa back into darkness and let the unknown man come to him. He would have to take a chance on Carla being the occupant of the bed. The high stakes would fully justify such ruthless action.

He started to move again when one of the seated men stood up abruptly. The red glow of his cigarette waved through the air as he pulled it from his lips and he said softly, "Damn this waiting. I need a drink."

Larren heard the man come towards him and automatically stepped back. A wineglass splintered under his descending heel and the crunching sound burst like a bomb in the absolute stillness.

The man uttered an exclamation of alarm as Larren was already springing forward to attack. The noise had precipitated the action and there was no time for thinking now. Larren did not even pause to curse the drunk who had left the glass on the floor as he hurled himself through the doorway and smashed the fist holding his automatic savagely at a point just to the left of the red pinpoint of light that marked the cigarette end. Most people are right-handed and as the cigarette was held low Larren judged that the blow should take the man hard in the stomach. The shuddering impact that ran up his arm and the agonized gasp as the man in front doubled up almost on top of him was solid proof that his reasoning had been correct.

However, as his victim fell he clutched wildly at Larren's hips and they overbalanced together. Larren heard the crash of a falling chair as the second man in the darkened room lurched to his feet and he clubbed desperately at his opponent's head. The very size of the man holding on to him told him that this was the fat companion of the man he had left unconscious outside. The fat man was practically helpless but his weight alone was enough to hinder Larren and prevent him from getting up.

Kicking furiously Larren succeeded in pushing the fat man away and he rolled frantically to one side as the sound of a clicking switch and a burst of light came simultaneously. In the first split seconds as the light filled the room Larren saw Savino standing by the door, an automatic jerking in his unsteady hand and his eyes staring wildly. The fat man still slobbered helplessly on the floor. The writhing, horrified form on the bed could only be Carla Valedri.

Savino swung his gun towards Larren and fired.

The shot was just a fraction too hurried and transformed the mirror above the dressing table that was behind Larren's head into a shower of flying fragments. Larren was cooler but he was firing from a more awkward angle on the floor. He took a snap shot at Savino and saw the Greek's lips peel back in a grimace of pain as his gun clattered to the floor. A scarlet streak like the swift slash from an invisible paint-brush had appeared along his forearm as he reeled back.

Larren scrambled to his feet. A tiny corner of his mind was still reminding him of the unknown man on the back porch and the fact that he was a clear target in the lighted room. He reached the doorway and plunged the room back into darkness with a sweeping motion of his hand. His momentum carried him on to close with Savino. Savino screamed a name.

"Christos. *Christos!*"

His voice was filled with panic and acted as a guide. Larren smashed his gun-heavy fist at the sound and connected with the young Greek's jaw. Savino fell away, the crash of his fall echoing solidly in the darkness. Larren could hear the fat man trying to get to his knees on the floor behind him and he kicked out hard in that direction. There was the barest hint of another movement from the doorway as his foot connected, a sound that was almost drowned by the thud of the fat man's body slumping back to the floor.

Larren took a silent pace to the left and froze.

There was utter silence now; and even Carla had stopped writhing on the bed. Larren strained his senses and wondered whether he had in fact heard that soft whisper of movement as the fat man collapsed. Had the unknown man from the back porch used that instant to slip into the room?

He remembered the name Savino had screamed: Christos. That could only be the unknown man whom he had not yet seen. Christos would have had plenty of time to get here during the fighting; time to enter silently and wait until he had separated friend from foe. Was he waiting now?

Larren's senses registered nothing in the blackness. He himself was motionless, controlling his breathing so even that made no sound. Then the feeling that he had experienced out on the dunes began to tingle his nerves again and he knew for sure.

The other man was somewhere in this

room, silently waiting for him to move. And the moment that he revealed his position that man would undoubtedly shoot. There was nothing he could do but wait; knowing that the other man was as deadly as he was himself — and knowing that the first one of them to move would die.

7

Duel of Silence

There was no sound to break the absolute stillness of the lonely beach-front villa; the murmur of the sea was too soft and distant to penetrate the time-weathered walls and there was no breeze to stir the branches of the pines that filled the grounds. There was not even a clock to disturb the tension with its ticking.

The sweat made Larren's palms itch until the irritation was almost unbearable as he strained his eyes and ears into the darkness. His heart was becoming more jittery with every nerve-tearing second, and there was a hollow sensation deep in his stomach that was gradually filling up with cold swirls of fear, rising up to choke him and drown the last shreds of his self control. He knew that Christos was somewhere in this room — but he did not know where.

He tried to place himself in the other man's position; if he had entered a darkened room of fighting men, how would he have acted? What position would he have taken up? The answer seemed obvious; he would have kept his back to a wall or corner, taking care to avoid the combatants until he knew which were friends and which were enemies. Was Christos in that corner nearest the door?

Larren directed all his senses into that one corner of the room but still he could not tell for sure. He had the feeling that the man was more likely to be there than anywhere else, for there had not been time for him to move very far into the room. But if he was there, was he standing, or kneeling — or perhaps even lying flat on the floor. Larren dared not take a chance of firing into that corner until he knew.

There was an abrupt noise in the darkness, a sharp gasping of released breath that filled the room and injected the heavy air with its own scent of terror. Larren almost jerked the trigger of his automatic towards the sound but instinct and icy control forced him to stay his hand. The breathing continued, frightened and uncomprehending, a harsh vibrant sound in the stillness.

It came from Carla Valedri who had been holding her breath as she lay bound and helpless on the bed, holding it until the rising pressure in her lungs had forced her to release it with an explosive gasp.

Larren realized that Christos too must have stayed his hand by instinct before he could have realized that the sound had come from Carla on the bed. The thought chilled the sweat on Larren's body and he had the eerie feeling that the other man was a reflection of his own character, a mirror of his own instincts and reflexes. He felt almost a kinship with this deadly enemy he had never seen. He and Christos were twins of the night, and the grim humour of fate had decreed that they must only meet in darkness, each with the sole object of out-waiting and killing the other.

Now that Carla had started breathing she was unable to stop and the ragged sound rasped upon the tension-filled air like a blunt saw upon raw flesh. Even the silence had been preferable to this and Larren felt an almost overpowering desire to scream or to blaze away with his automatic, to kill or die — anything to break the awful strain. It required a fantastic effort of will to continue to regulate his own soundless breathing and he knew that soon he would have to make some move. He could feel his control beginning to slip away.

Surely the other man must feel it too!

Only a few minutes had passed since the agonizing silence had clamped down, but already it seemed an eternity. The swirls of fear were spinning faster in Larren's stomach and threatening to engulf him in panic at any time. Then everything exploded at once.

There was a brief impression of movement from the floor to Larren's right and Larren swung his automatic towards it. But Christos was even faster. A second automatic roared twice from a spot several feet to the left of the corner where Larren had half expected the other man to be, and then there was the ugly splat of bullets tearing into flesh in the same instant. On the floor the body of the fat man whom Larren had kicked unconscious jerked and twisted with the impact; his first stirring movement to recovering consciousness had also been his last.

The two shots had been fired from a position low against the wall and Larren knew that the other man had been kneeling as he waited for that first sound to mark a target. However, Christos had already realized his mistake and even as Larren fired back the mystery man was catapulting himself forward. Larren heard the crash as the other man hurled himself bodily out of the room through the still open door, and he knew that he had missed.

Savagely Larren slammed another shot through the doorway, cursing as he realized that Christos would already be rolling clear. He knew better than to take the suicide risk of following his enemy through that narrow gap, but he also knew that he had to get out of the bedroom fast. He knew the location of the window on the far side of the room from his brief visit earlier in the evening and he sprang towards it.

He leapt over the body of the fat man and reached the window in three running strides. His outstretched hand encountered the closed curtains that had kept the room in such utter darkness and he tore them aside. The windows were closed but he had anticipated that, for the room could not have been so soundproof had they been open. The windowsill was low and he kicked out expertly at the foot of the windows where the two frames opened. Both sides crashed apart and Larren leapt through into the grounds.

He sprinted away from the window, swerving into the pines and heading for the rear of the villa. The cold spur of fear still urged him on for it was quite possible that Christos had doubled back into the bedroom and might even now be taking practised aim at his fleeing back. However, no shot came, and he reached the rear of the villa without mishap.

Here he waited, striving to modulate

the over-fast pounding of his heart. Now that he had relaxed the iron control he had exercised over his breathing he was panting hard and he found it impossible to regain that control again. He wiped the sweat from his palms down the thighs of his trousers, momentarily changing hands with his automatic as he dried each palm in turn; then he forced himself to move slowly towards the back entrance to the villa.

As he moved his brain was already ticking over at a staccato pace, again attempting to foresee the other man's movements. Christos had not doubled back into the bedroom so that would leave him with three courses of action: he could continue to wait inside the villa in the hope that Larren would re-enter; he could race outside by one of the other exits and attempt to circle through the grounds and come upon Larren from the rear; or finally he could simply make his escape and flee. It all depended on the odds at stake and the amount of loyalty he owed to his companions. Larren had no way of assessing either factor and so it was impossible to guess at what Christos would do.

Larren stepped up on to the back porch and felt much safer as his body was drowned by the inky blackness. He stood there listening; reluctant to enter the building again, but at a loss to decide upon what other course to take. Then abruptly he heard a car engine reverberating from the front of the villa.

He sprang down from the porch and sprinted wildly through the grounds, circling the large, sprawling house through the shading pines. The car snarled into full life long before he could reach the drive and he heard the wheels spin in the gravel as the clutch was released and the vehicle roared away. He reached the front of the villa just in time to see the rear lights disappearing through the gateway that opened on to the main road.

He cursed sourly, but at the same time he was aware of a deep sense of inner relief. He had faced dangerous men before, but never one who commanded quite so much respect within him as the unknown, unseen man whom Savino had called Christos. His mouth still retained the unpleasant taste of fear from their encounter in the darkened room, and he did not particularly want to tangle with the man again.

He went back inside the villa. The man with the dark glasses who had originally stood guard on the porch still lay there in a crumpled heap, and Larren paused only to make sure that he was still fully unconscious before moving on. He returned to the bedroom and switched on the light.

It only needed a brief glance to show that the unfortunate fat man was stone dead. He lay on his stomach and face with twin pools of blood growing beneath his gross corpse. Christos had spaced his shots and one had taken him high up just below the armpit while the second had hit low in the stomach. Larren failed to suppress the shudder that came as he remembered that those shots had been meant for him.

Savino still sprawled on his back, his chest moving slowly and his eyes closed. The blood was growing sticky on the creasing wound along his right forearm and there were bright spots like a red rash on the rolled-up sleeve of his white shirt.

Larren turned his attention towards the bed and saw Carla's dark eyes staring at him wildly. A white handkerchief covered her mouth and most of her body was hidden beneath a thin white sheet, only one bare shoulder showed where the sheet had slipped as she struggled to raise herself up.

There was still fear in her eyes as Larren moved towards the bed and he said quietly, "It's all right, Carla. It's me, Simon. Everybody else has gone and I'm here to help you."

He remembered that he was still holding an automatic and slipped the weapon into his pocket. He fumbled with the knot in the handkerchief behind her head, and when he released it she thankfully spat a second, screwed-up, handkerchief out of her mouth.

She choked for a moment and then managed to speak.

"Th — thanks, Simon. I — I thought

I was going to choke."

Larren smiled. "Just take it easy for a moment. You can talk when you get your breath back."

He had to pull away the flimsy sheet in order to release the cords that secured her hands and ankles and found that she was completely naked underneath. He guessed that Savino and Co. had simply rolled her up in a sheet from her own bed when they had carried her out of her hotel room. The smooth, nude lines of her limbs and the swelling, still frightened movements of her breasts made his pulses race, and he was glad when she rolled over on to her face so that he could untie her. Right now he wanted to get away from the villa before Christos could return with reinforcements, and he did not welcome any distractions.

His fingers wrestled deftly with knots and although they were pulled tight he soon had them undone. Carla rolled back to face him and sat up slowly. She was still trembling as she rubbed her sore wrists and her dark eyes gazed nervously into his face. For the first time he realized how very dark and liquid those soft eyes really were, they were wide and exciting beneath black, glistening lashes; almost as exciting as her naked breasts and quivering body.

She said huskily, "What's it all about, Simon? Why was I kidnapped? Why are you here?"

Larren realized that she was most probably unaware of her father's present project and consequently had no idea of why she had been kidnapped. He also realized that if it was at all possible then he still had to act the part of the uncomprehending lover.

He made a vague gesture with his hands and answered.

"I don't know. I went back to your hotel because I wanted to talk to you again and found you missing. I knew that Savino was highly jealous about tonight and I thought that he might have turned nasty, so I came over here to see if he did know anything about it. It seems that was right — but I never expected all th gunplay."

"But you had a gun of your own!"

There was a note of suspicion in her tone and Larren was glad he had an honest answer.

"I took it away from the man they left to watch the front door," he said. And then to forestall any further questions he added quickly, "Look, we'd better get you dressed and get out of here, just in case the man who got away decides to come back."

The thought had obviously not occurred to Carla for her body gave an abrupt shudder at the idea. "Try the wardrobe," she said shakily. "There might be a dressing-gown or something in there."

Larren moved around the bed towards the wardrobe and pulled open the door. There were a few gaily-coloured men's shirts on the hangers and other odd items of beachwear on the shelves. There was no dressing-gown but there was a large bath-robe which he took down and offered to Carla.

"How about this? It'll cover you decently until I can get you back to your hotel."

Her composure was beginning to

recover and she managed a smile. "That will do fine," she said. She stood up and turned her back to him, and he had to suppress the urge to kiss the nape of her neck as he slipped the robe around her.

Carla turned to face him and as she did so her gaze rested for a moment on the ugly sight of the dead man on the floor. She looked away quickly and her face was white.

Larren said quietly, "Go and wait for me in the next room while I try and find out who he is. I won't be a minute." He tried to inject distaste into his tone as he spoke, it was imperative that she did not realize how cold and efficient he could be.

Carla was only too willing and obediently allowed him to lead her outside. He switched on the light in the next room and made her sit down while he returned to the bedroom. He half closed the door behind him so that she could not watch him work and swiftly went through the fat man's pockets. He discovered another automatic and a wallet full of 100 drachma notes, but there was nothing to reveal the man's identity. Scowling he left the corpse and crossed over to Savino.

Savino was in his shirtsleeves but his jacket hung on the back of a nearby chair; Larren went through it and in the inside pocket he unearthed a second full wallet. Again it was stuffed with crisp red 100 drachma notes, but this time there was something else of far more interest. The wallet contained a photograph of a young man in his late twenties. Larren stared at the dark handsome features of the smiling man and knew that he had seen that face before. The face was southern European, probably Italian, and as the word Italian flickered through Larren's mind he knew who the man was. The picture had appeared in several recent papers and there was no doubt in Larren's mind that this was Paola Castel: Carla Valedri's brother and Angelo Valedri's son, and also the chemist who had discovered the antidote for the killer drug Ameytheline.

What was it doing in Savino's pocket? Where was the connection between Savino and Castel?

Larren turned the snapshot over and saw some faded pencil marks on the back. He read them with difficulty; one word and a combination of letters and numbers. ROMA A9986B. He stared at it thoughtfully. Was it a telephone number? or a Rome car number? Quite suddenly he knew that it must be the number of Castel's car — the car in which the young chemist had died, in an accident that might not have been an accident.

Could Castel's death have been murder? And could Savino or one of his colleagues have been responsible?

Larren knew that it was a strong possibility, but there was no time to think about it now. He was beginning to realize that Savino and his friends must have been waiting for someone else to arrive and take Carla off their hands, for they could not have kept her here at the villa indefinitely. And whoever they were waiting for could arrive at any time. Also Christos could return, and he had no idea of the whereabouts of the man named Dimitri who owned this villa and whom he assumed must also be mixed up in the night's events. Grimly he slipped the snapshot of Castel into his own pocket and then rejoined Carla.

She stood up unsteadily.

"Who — who was he, Simon?"

"I don't know. I looked through his pockets but I couldn't find anything. He was a bit messy and — " He let the sentence trail off sheepishly as though he had been unable to face the task and had given up half-way through.

Carla took a step towards him and he moved forward and put his arms round her. "I'll take you home now," he said. "We can talk about it later."

She nodded and he kept one arm tightly around her as he led her out of the back door of the villa and hurried her along the beach. She stumbled several times in the soft sand as they made their way back to his car and he kept repeating words of encouragement in her ear. However, by the time they reached the parked Renault the worst effects of her ordeal were wearing off and she was able to smile and complain about the cold draught that was circling up below the loose bath-robe.

They were both silent as they drove back into Athens and Carla pressed close up against Larren's body as he continued to keep one arm about her shoulders. He handled the car expertly with one hand and soon they were again nearing the centre of the city. It was nearing dawn now and Larren found that he was having difficulty in keeping his eyes open. Long nights were nothing new to him, but tonight had been particularly hectic and he would be glad of an opportunity to relax.

At last the lighted frontage of the Hotel Tripolis appeared again and Larren wearily stopped the car. The night clerk was still dozing behind his desk in the foyer and they walked past him to the lift. They were silent all the way up to the second floor and then moved quietly to Carla's room. Carla switched on the lights and Larren closed the door.

Without a word Carla moved to the small cabinet and poured two stiff whiskies. She handed one to Larren and they both drained the glasses. Then she said huskily, "That's better, Simon. I feel more like a woman now. Being carted about in the nude and bundled up in a sheet isn't exactly the best way of maintaining your dignity." Her face darkened and she added, "Some of the remarks those swine made made me feel unclean just to listen to them."

Larren said, "I'm sorry. I should have got there earlier."

The smile came back. "Please don't apologize. I'm more than grateful that you came when you did."

Larren said slowly, "What did Savino and his friends really want? There seemed to be too many men ready to help him for it to be merely a question of his own personal jealousy."

Carla looked blank. "I don't know, Simon. I just don't know."

"How much do you know about Savino? How long have you known him?"

Carla moved closer and she trembled a little as she answered. "Not now, Simon; please don't ask questions now. I'm so tired and confused that I just can't think straight."

"All right." He was aware of the compelling magnetism of her body and could not resist the appeal in her eyes. He went on slowly. "Perhaps I'd better go and let you get some sleep."

Her hands caught at his shoulders. "No, Simon. Please don't go — not tonight."

His eyes were drawn irresistibly into the folds of her robe where the soft breasts rose and fell in the dark shadows. He raised his gaze to meet her eyes and said quietly, "What about that clerk who might throw you out tomorrow?"

She pulled his mouth down to her lips and the rising urgency of her own desires flowed into his body to fire the flames of his own lust. "To hell with him," she gasped as she strained against him. "Tonight I need you, Simon — in more ways than one." Her mouth was fierce and demanding, blending and moving against his own. He answered her kiss and then all control was lost and there was no retreat.

Somehow she wriggled her shoulders clear of the bathrobe and let it fall to the floor. She pulled his hand to her breast and clamped it hard against her. Now the frightened girl who had merely wanted him to stay as a means of protection was gone and the aroused nymphomaniac was in her place.

"You can't leave me now, Simon. Not tonight. You can't! *You can't!*"

Larren could feel the swelling of her breasts under his palm with the hot pulse of her heartbeat vibrating through his fingers, and he knew that she was right. When he was at last able to free his mouth from her kisses and speak he said hoarsely, "I'm not leaving you, Carla. Tonight you're mine."

8

Kyros Island

When Larren awoke the next morning, or rather late the next day, Carla still lay in his arms in the wide bed. He must have stirred and disturbed her as he awakened for she opened her eyes in almost the same moment and lay looking up at him. There was a half smile on her lips and obvious traces of contentment and satisfaction in the way she snuggled closer against him. Her raven black hair spread in shining waves over the pillow and her dark eyes regarded him inquiringly. Larren said softly, "Well, what now?"

Her fingers lightly stroked his bare chest.

"What do you mean by what now?"

"What happens now? We must do something about last night — go to the police or something."

Her smile faded a little and she stopped

stroking his chest. "I don't like that idea," she said doubtfully. "I don't want my picture in the papers and all Athens talking about how I was kidnapped in the nude. If I had been kidnapped with some clothes on I wouldn't mind so much — but this way the papers will write it up from a sexy angle and I shall be the subject of a lot of dirty little thoughts in a lot of sordid little minds. I'd rather forget it."

Larren tried to appear shocked. "But a man was killed last night!"

"I know." She pulled herself up slightly so that she was half sitting and half leaning over him. "That's another reason why I don't want the police involved." She smiled almost sadly and went on. "I'm sorry, Simon, but I haven't got a very pure reputation in Athens, and a lot of people will be very cynical when we explain that you were more or less defending my honour. They believe I sold my honour long ago. Our story could be very easily misbelieved and you might be in serious trouble."

Larren would have been quite happy

to accept that view and be done, but he had to say the sort of thing that would be expected of a bewildered lover who more by luck than judgement had been able to rectify an unpleasant situation.

With a well-feigned note of dithering he said vaguely, "But surely we can't just forget it."

Carla smiled and kissed him gently. "I don't see why not, darling. I think they came very much the worst off so we can hardly harbour any thoughts of revenge, and as I don't see how the police can trace anything back to us there is no reason why we should stir up trouble for ourselves."

Larren tried to sound dubious. "I suppose you're right," he offered hesitantly.

"Of course I'm right." Carla kissed him again and this time the kiss was a long one; a soft, warm, pleading kiss that was calculated to turn any man's thoughts from any subject under the sun — except one.

Larren allowed her to have her way and gave himself up to a few moments of sweet luxury. He was aware that he might

131

have been in quite an awkward spot if Carla had been agreeable to calling in the police, but he had been fairly sure that he was on safe ground. Carla was her father's daughter, and even though she may not know the details of his present operation it was a certainty that he had instilled her with a deep distrust of the police.

When at last they relaxed and she was settling back in the hollow of his arm again Larren decided that it was time that he took the initiative.

He said thoughtfully, "If you don't want to call the police, Carla, don't you think that it would be a good idea for you to leave Athens until Savino has had plenty of time to cool down. After last night he'll probably be more enraged at you than ever and he might try to get at you again. Isn't there somewhere that you could go and hide up for a spell?"

As he spoke he wondered whether he had made his gamble too soon, but it was too late now. He kept his eyes averted and tried to appear casual as he waited for her answer.

"As a matter of fact there is." She murmured the words as though thinking out loud. "My father owns the ideal place. He has a villa on a small island in the Aegean — Kyros."

Larren hardly dared to hope as he replied. "In that case I should definitely advise you to take a short holiday out there until this thing blows over. Your friend Savino doesn't strike me as the kind of man to accept a blow to his pride without some attempt at retaliation." He paused there for a moment and then added slowly. "The only drawback is that if you do leave Athens then I shall have no chance of ever seeing you again." He let a note of doubt creep into his voice as though he was already beginning to regret the suggestion that she should leave, and again he dared not look at her directly as he waited for her to speak. Any small hint of eagerness might arouse her suspicions now, and there were too many lives dependent upon persuading her to take him out to Kyros for him to risk that; lives that were yielding all over Europe to the horror of the red death.

She took a long time in answering, and Larren felt a cold, sinking sensation in his stomach. Had he rushed her too soon and allowed her to sense how important it was for him to reach her father's island? He wasn't sure, but slowly he became aware that she was watching him closely and waiting for him to turn his head.

Slowly, casually he let his head roll to one side and faced up to her. She was smiling seductively. "Why don't you come to Kyros with me, Simon? It's lovely out there on the Aegean; there's nothing to do except swim in the sea and laze on the beach in the sun. I wear the tiniest bikini and occasionally you could make love to me on the sand." Her eyes gleamed with a subtle challenge. "Would you like that, Simon?"

Larren smiled and stretched up one arm to encircle her bare shoulders. He pulled her closer and tasted her lips as he answered. "I'd love it. I've got another three weeks to spend in Greece and right now they can keep the Acropolis for all the other tourists. I'll settle for Kyros — and you."

The kiss became fiercer as she began to respond and her ever-hungry body began to tremble against him with desire.

"Prove it to me, Simon." She moaned through seeking lips. "Prove it to me now." Her voice rose desperately. "Now, Simon! *NOW!*"

★ ★ ★

The island of Kyros was a two-and-a-half-hour journey by a fast motor launch from the small boat harbour at Athens, and it was late in the afternoon when Larren saw its steep white cliffs rising from the pure blue of the Aegean for the first time. Above the cliffs the long grass on the gentle slopes was a dusty olive-green, broken by rugged scatterings of boulders and bare rock, and on the highest point overlooking the sea a pinnacle of natural rock, bleached by sun, wind and spray, rose like an ivory shrine to the searing blue sky.

The launch was the property of Carla Valedri who stood at the wheel with her legs splayed to maintain her balance and

135

her black hair streaming freely in the slipstream. She was wearing a pair of bright red shorts and a brief matching sun-top which she had donned in the small cabin of the launch as soon as she came aboard. Larren, in casual slacks and open shirt, was standing just behind her and admiring the way she handled the speeding craft at full throttle.

Carla glanced back at him and gestured with one hand towards the pinnacle of rock high on the cliff top. "See that, Simon," she shouted happily. "That's the sanctuary of Poseidon; there are steps cut in the landward side of that pointed rock where the priests of ancient Greece once climbed up to throw down offerings to the sea god. It's pretty small compared to the other temples and sanctuaries scattered along the coastline of the mainland, but its worth a visit. I'll take you up there tomorrow."

By the time she had finished speaking they were almost underneath the sheer white cliffs and she swung the launch round in a creaming white circle that put the island on their starboard bow instead of directly ahead. They raced along the line of the cliffs for a few moments and then abruptly the high rock face dipped and gave way to a perfect little bay; there was even a yellow-gold beach and a small jetty.

Carla looked back and shouted again. "This is where we land, Simon. It's the only beach on the island, all the other sides are sheer cliffs."

She headed the launch for the small jetty and Larren saw that there were already two other fast-looking launches moored close to the beach. Beyond the strip of clean sand the ground became grassy and rugged again, rising steeply to where a sprawling white villa with gleaming walls and square, modern angles was tucked into a natural fold and shaded by olives, pines and dark, slender cypresses. Larren's practised gaze was carefully recording details as he surveyed the island, and when his attention returned to the jetty they were almost there and Carla was coasting to a stop. A reception committee of two hard-faced, hard-muscled men in slacks and sweat shirts had already arrived to meet them.

Carla called gaily to the leader of the two, a blunt-faced man with cropped hair and stony grey eyes, and he deftly caught the mooring rope she tossed into his hands. He pulled the drifting launch close into the jetty and then handed the rope to his companion as he reached down to help her step up on to the wooden jetty. "Your father will be pleased to see you, Carla," he said flatly. Then his gaze turned to Larren and he demanded bluntly, "Who's your friend?"

Carla laughed. "Don't sound so distrustful, Bruno. This is Simon and I owe him quite a lot." Turning back to Larren she went on. "Simon, this is Bruno, he's my father's right-hand man. What he actually does I've never quite been able to find out, but Father seems to find him indispensable."

Larren acted as though he lacked the sense to detect the other man's antagonism and thrust out his hand as he reached the jetty. "Hello," he said amiably. "Glad to meet you."

Doubtfully Bruno accepted the gesture, and his grip was hard and short. He drew his hand back almost immediately.

Turning to Carla he said brusquely, "We had better go up to the villa."

He led the way while Carla and Larren followed, the remaining man stayed behind to secure the launch. The sun was hot on Larren's back as he walked up the beach and for a moment he could almost forget the surly man in front and wish that he really was here for an idyllic interlude with the handsome woman by his side. Then the sand gave way to thickening grass and the bright sunlight suddenly darted back at his eyes in a silver flash from the ground. The flicker only lasted for a fraction of a second but Larren found the spot again as they walked past. A slender wire lay slack and almost hidden in the grass. Larren knew that after dark that wire would be tightened up and raised several inches above the ground, and it would be carrying a lethal, high voltage charge of electricity. Then, as if to drive home the point that he was on highly dangerous soil, he heard the short, deep-throated bark of a large dog coming from behind the luxurious villa. His unsmiling mouth tightened a fraction and he concentrated his thoughts again on his mission.

There were two tall Doric columns flanking the wide entrance to the villa, and Larren felt his heart pulse just a little faster as he climbed the smooth marble steps between them. Carla pressed close to his side and smiled at him with the pleasure of a child showing off its favourite toy. Larren had to answer her smile and look around him as though he was suitably impressed.

They passed through wide open, glass-fronted doors and Larren found himself in a large carpeted room which, apart from the wide-railed staircase on the right-hand side, could easily have done service as the luxury lounge of a top grade hotel. It had the same expensive, but not quite lived-in look, and Larren had the feeling that it had been furnished by someone with more money than taste. A heavy, glittering chandelier hung in the centre of the room and on either side two slow fans were fitted into the ceiling, each revolving silently and making hardly any impression on the still air.

Then a door opened near the foot of the staircase and a tall, ageing man in a light-weight white suit came into the room. He walked with a pronounced limp but the most striking thing about him was the dark, deep-set gleam of his eyes. He stared at them without speaking.

Bruno stepped to one side and Carla ran forward to throw her arms round the old man's neck.

"Papa!" She cried impulsively, and she kissed him on the lips. The old man did not respond and she drew back uncertainly. "Papa," she used the Italian term of her childhood again. "Why are you scowling?"

The tall old man looked down at her and managed to spare her a quick, reassuring smile. Then he looked up at Larren and the smile vanished.

"Who is your new friend, Carla?" He asked softly.

Carla smiled. "This is Simon, he

practically saved my life in Athens last night."

Then she turned to Larren and formally introduced him to the man who was using the vital Ameytheline antidote to blackmail the British Government, and callously allowing hundreds of the victims of the drug to die; the man whom Larren had come to kill.

She said brightly, "Simon, this is my father — Angelo Valedri."

9

Night Callers

Valedri hesitated for several long-drawn moments, and despite his outward air of smiling calm Simon Larren's heart began to thump just a fraction faster than normal. Then Valedri limped slowly towards him and held out his hand.

"My friend," he said pleasantly. "If you have been of service to my daughter then I am most grateful — and you are most welcome."

Larren accepted the offered handshake and found the grip light but firm. The deep-set eyes regarded him keenly from the dark, smooth face and he knew that the man was only acting to please his daughter. Angelo Valedri was suspicious as hell.

Larren continued to smile and answered courteously. "Thank you. I hope we are not causing any inconvenience by arriving so suddenly, but after last night we felt that it would be best for Carla to leave Athens for a while, and she insisted that I come with her."

Valedri released his hand. "What exactly did happen last night?" he demanded quietly.

It was Carla who told him. Larren listened as she recounted everything from the moment he had gate-crashed Dimitri's party to the moment they had landed on Kyros. She talked quickly and eagerly and constantly doubled back over events to bring back details she had missed. Now that she was safely out of Savino's reach she had left all fears and uncertainty behind and only the excitement remained.

Angelo Valedri heard her through without interruption, and so did the stony-eyed Bruno who now stood discreetly to one side. Larren wanted to study the two men and estimate their reactions but he dared not show that amount of interest and forced himself to watch Carla instead. Then gradually he became aware that there was yet another silent listener to Carla's story, and he turned his gaze slowly to the top of the wide staircase.

A woman stood there; an obviously young and well-curved woman in a trim one-piece swimsuit of yellow silk. Her head and shoulders were in shadow but there could be no doubt about the desirability of that fine young body. Larren tried to distinguish her face but it was impossible, and when he realized that she was watching him in return he looked away.

Carla finished her recital and looked proudly from Valedri to Larren. Valedri had to say something but again his eyes betrayed the false sincerity in his tone as he spoke.

"It seems that I owe you more than my thanks, my friend," he offered slowly. "The hospitality of Kyros is yours for as long as you wish to stay."

Larren murmured his thanks, and at the same time wondered what really was going through Valedri's mind. There was no doubt that the ex-racketeer and killer was genuinely fond of his daughter, but he appeared to show no sign of alarm over her kidnapping and no hint of anger towards Savino and his friends. Nothing showed in his eyes except the distrust that he felt for his guest. Larren had the feeling that he did not believe that his daughter had been in any serious danger. Then, before his thoughts could bring him to any conclusion, there was an interruption from the staircase.

"Didn't I warn you about that young Greek, Carla darling? A handsome young man with a fast sports car *and* money was just too good to be true. Only decrepit old men can afford both."

The voice was feminine and so pleasant that the soft hint of cynicism was almost smoothed over. Larren looked up to see the woman in the yellow swimsuit descending the stairs with one hand on the rail. She was smiling and her face was lovely enough to match her body.

Carla looked towards her and laughed. "Antonella, you only say that because you were jealous." She turned back to Larren and added quickly, "Simon, this is Antonella, she's Father's friend." The mischievous intonation she placed behind the word "friend" made it plain that the woman was Valedri's mistress.

Larren acknowledged the introduction and Antonella gave him a brief nod of greeting. Now that she had moved down into the light Larren could see that her bare legs, arms and shoulders were deeply tanned and almost glowed with health. Her hair was parted into two sweeping bronze-red waves that came well forward on either side of her face and then curved upwards in an attractive curl. The colour of her eyes was undefinable but her mouth was full and moistly enticing. However, there was something about the bone structure of her face that struck a puzzling note in Larren's mind; she was definitely not Italian and equally definitely not Greek. He could not place her nationality and for some reason that bothered him.

Her voice gave him no clue as she turned back to Carla and said, "Perhaps I was just a little bit jealous. But now I'm glad that he was your lover and not mine. I wonder why he wanted to kidnap you though?"

Valedri answered. "I am a rich man, Antonella, perhaps this Savino hoped to hold her to ransom."

"I don't think it was that. I think he was just jealous because I left him." Carla sounded almost hurt at the suggestion that it might have been otherwise.

Valedri smiled and patted her on the shoulder. "Perhaps you are right, your beauty could make many men do foolish things. However, there is no more need for you to worry. I shall attend to your friend Savino myself."

Only an experienced man like Larren could have detected the slight note of menace in Valedri's last sentence, and he felt almost a pang of pity for Savino. Valedri had killed callously to order during his apprenticeship with Murder Incorporated, so there could be little doubt that he would hesitate to carry out his threat should the opportunity arise.

There was a moment of silence and then Valedri went on. "Antonella, will you accept my duty as a host and show our guest to his room. I think perhaps the room next to Bruno's will be suitable."

He faced Larren and added, "You will excuse me won't you? but I should like to speak privately with Carla."

"Of course," Larren assured him agreeably. He knew full well that Valedri simply wanted him out of the way until he had had a chance to question Carla more thoroughly, and he had not missed the significant fact that he was to be accommodated where the watchful Bruno could keep him under constant surveillance — but there was nothing else he could do.

Carla gave him a parting smile, and then on Antonella's invitation Larren turned to follow her up the staircase. From his advantage point immediately behind and below her he could again admire the smooth, tanned lines of her body and the lithe movement of her hips beneath the revealing swimsuit; but the last thing he wanted was another source of distraction and he forced the thoughts they aroused out of his mind.

At the top of the staircase Antonella led him along a short corridor that opened out on to a balcony through tall french windows, but half-way along she stopped to open one of the bedroom doors that lined each wall. She stood back to let him enter and he walked into a large room furnished in panelled walnut. A double bed filled the centre of the room, the floor was softly covered with fawn carpeting and the view from the open window overlooked the beach.

Larren turned to thank her and found that she had entered the room behind him and had closed the door. She was leaning against it with her arms at her sides and was staring at him with unflinching eyes. Larren answered her gaze and found that he still couldn't decide upon what colour her eyes were.

She said calmly, "The bathroom is through that door on your left, Simon. There's a shower there and it's all fitted with hot and cold water so you should be quite comfortable." She paused meaningly and then added softly. "I suppose your name is Simon — or is it?"

Larren was startled, and he made no attempt to hide the fact.

He said sharply, "What's that supposed to mean?"

Antonella raised one hand and casually patted her bronze-red hair into place. The movement made her breasts lift negligently beneath the yellow silk and Larren had no doubt that she knew exactly what she was doing. "Your name may or may not be Simon," she explained. "But that is really immaterial. The point is that no naive tourist stupid enough to drive his car into a gatepost would have the resources to deal with men like Savino and his friends. If you did in fact take Carla away from them then it was by design, not by chance; and it must have been achieved by skill and planning, not by luck and accident." Her tone became condescending, like a patient teacher explaining the ABC to a child. "That seems to leave us with one simple question, doesn't it. Who and what are you?"

Larren took a pace towards her and demanded coldly, "Are you trying to suggest that Carla and I are lying for some reason?"

151

Antonella laughed. "Don't bring poor Carla into it, she's too sex-happy to think of anything else. As long as you can keep her purring that way she'll trust you as much as she trusted Savino, and for all she could tell you may turn out to be just as bad. Carla would sleep with the devil if he proved capable."

Larren found it easy to feign anger. "You seem to have a pretty nasty mind," he snapped. "Perhaps you can dream up a good reason that I might have for lying to her?"

"Perhaps I can. And perhaps Angelo can dream up one or two for himself."

It was a threat, and yet it wasn't; Larren watched her face and sensed that it had been said merely to test his reaction.

"If you think you have anything to tell Valedri then perhaps it's best if you run and tell him," he retorted grimly.

Antonella laughed softly. "Don't worry about Angelo, he can reason things out for himself. He's a very shrewd man." She moved away from the door until she was standing close and facing him. "Let's start again shall we, I'm curious to know who you are."

He returned the level stare in those undefinable eyes. "The name is Simon Larren, I'm spending a three-week holiday in Greece, and last night I was fortunate enough to meet Carla and help her out of a nasty spot. Is there anything else you want to know?"

She shook her head slowly. "It's no good, Mr. Larren, your cover story is just too weak."

Larren groaned aloud. "There is no cover story. I just don't understand what you're talking about."

Antonella sighed sadly and moved back to the door. "I wish you'd tell me," she insisted. "I simply hate puzzles." She gave him a taunting look that was almost a gesture of sympathy and finished. "I suppose you must be pretty good to have dealt with Savino, but I'm afraid you're going to be out of your depth here on Kyros. Angelo can practically smell a phoney a mile away. You really shouldn't have come." She gave her hair a delicate pat again, making sure to repeat the teasing breast movement that went with it. Larren knew that she was laughing at him despite her failure to extract any real information. She said lightly, "I'll leave you until dinner, Mr. Larren. Try and think up a good story for Angelo." Then she opened the door and left him with a last coaxing smile. "If you do decide to talk, my room is at the end of the corridor."

Larren drew a deep breath and then turned and walked across to the open window. He stared down across the beach without really seeing it and found that he was unable to relax the sudden tightness of his mouth. He badly needed a drink but there was nothing available.

The red-haired beauty in the yellow swimsuit was far more intelligent than any ordinary mistress had a right to be and he found it hard to visualize her simply as Valedri's bed-mate. Whatever she was he knew that she was dangerous and would have to be closely watched. And she was completely right about one thing — his cover story was too weak. In fact it was hardly a cover at all. He swore softly to himself and began to wish that he had taken more time to prepare himself for this mission. The fact that the red death was costing twenty lives a day no longer seemed to justify the way he had rushed headlong into the job; for if he failed now through lack of the normal precautions those others would continue to die anyway. And if Valedri detected any basis for his suspicions then Larren knew that he would be murdered, and there was no failure more final than that.

He was beginning to realize now that his biggest obstacle had not been simply to get to Kyros, but to remain here long enough to achieve any purpose. He had been forced to come unarmed, for Valedri and his men would have spotted any weapon straight away, and his only course was to wait his opportunity to eliminate Valedri and escape with the antidote. Now it seemed that unless Carla's testimony could convince her father that he was the lucky amateur he claimed to be he would have no chance to wait for any such opportunity, and he would probably be killed out of hand.

Abruptly he stopped dwelling upon the blackest implications of his position and told himself grimly that he had known the odds before he had started; now he could only trust in his ability to bluff his way through. The old gleam came back into his grey-green eyes and this time details began to register as he stared down the beach. He could see three men, all strangers, lounging around in the shade, and together with Bruno and the other man who had met them at the jetty that made at least five men whom Valedri had at his disposal. He knew the location of one trip wire and he knew that the guard dogs were most probably chained at the back of the house during the day. Every detail helped him to add up the odds in Valedri's favour and a complete knowledge of those odds could well save his life. He filed away full mental pictures of the beach and the layout of the surrounding cliffs and then at last he turned away from the window.

His palms were damp and he decided

that he might as well take a shower before dinner.

* * *

It was Carla who eventually came up to his room to tell him that dinner was served. In the meantime one of Valedri's men had brought up his single suitcase from the launch and he had changed into his light grey suit and added a dark tie. Carla's manner was hesitant and awkward and Larren knew that she was thinking hard over whatever her father had said. However, despite his inner feelings, he looked like a man without a care in the world as he followed her out of the room.

The dining-room lay beyond the door at the foot of the staircase and he found Valedri, Bruno and Antonella already seated round the large table. It was growing dusk now and the wavering flames from a tall, delicately-wrought pair of candelabrum danced over the pure white linen and gleaming silverware. Valedri greeted him affably,

Bruno merely nodded, and Antonella gave him a knowing smile.

Larren acknowledged their gestures and took his place at the table. Carla sat next to him, pulling her chair deliberately close to him and glaring defensively across the table at Valedri. The friction between father and daughter was so marked that Larren wondered how he could possibly pretend to ignore it.

A male servant brought in the food and Larren noted automatically that despite his pressed white uniform and quiet efficiency the man looked well capable of doing double duty as an extra strong arm man. That made six men at Valedri's disposal. Surely there could not be many more!

The meal began in silence with an excellent but unidentifiable soup with a sharp, peppery tang, and was followed by a course of fish. The fish had been fried whole and although its flavour was beyond reproach Larren found it somewhat disconcerting to have its one visible and wide open eye gazing up at him as he ate. His glass was kept constantly filled with the bitter retzina wine that is the favourite aperitif of Greece.

There was no conversation except for occasional murmured pleasantries between courses and Larren was permanently aware of Carla smouldering beside him. It was clear that Valedri had expressed his doubts and interrogated her closely, and had aroused within her a strong sense of uncertainty and resentment. However, Larren took comfort in the fact that he was still being treated as a guest, for that in itself indicated that Valedri must have accepted her testimony on his behalf.

Discreetly he attempted to sum up his table companions as he ate, but he was unable to reach any concrete conclusions. Bruno, now clad in a black tuxedo, had not yet uttered a single word that might have provided a clue to his background. While Antonella, now wearing a ravishing yellow gown — yellow was obviously her favourite colour — contented herself with sparing him momentary flashes of that insinuating smile. Valedri still wore his white suit and seemed intent on nothing more serious than enjoying his food.

A dish of pineapple slices in rich cream and then small cups of sweet black Turkish coffee finished off the meal. As he drank his coffee Larren had an opportunity to lean back and casually observe his host. Valedri was sixty-three years old and carried himself well, his sleek black hair was still thick and plentiful and there was nothing in his dark face to show that he had spent twenty-three of those years in an Italian prison. Apart from the limp that had remained as a permanent legacy of his unsuccessful attempt to rob a bank that had put him inside he showed no outward traces of his past. At the moment he looked more paternal than anything else as he sat at the head of his table, and it was hard to believe that he was callously holding back the Ameytheline antidote in a cold-blooded game of blackmail.

Finally Carla rose to her feet and invited Larren to join her in the larger room. They took their second cup of coffee with them and Larren was glad to get away from that silent table with its atmosphere of hidden tensions.

However, Carla had carried some of that atmosphere with her and nothing seemed able to dispel it. She played a few jazzy records and talked vaguely about the island and the villa. None of the other members of the household seemed inclined to join them and Larren found her unenthusiastic conversation more of a strain than anything else. He sensed that although she must have defended him from her father she no longer fully trusted him. She seemed to be unable to make up her mind whether to question him or not, and then abruptly she decided that she was going to bed. She explained that she was very tired after the previous night, but Larren knew that she simply wanted to be alone to think things out.

He escorted her up to her bedroom and lingered to kiss her goodnight, but this time there was no clamouring response in her ripe young body and that in itself was a sure sign that she was badly worried. He still kissed her fiercely, holding her against him like a bewildered lover who could not comprehend what was wrong.

Finally she pulled away and complained again that she was tired. There was nothing Larren could do except leave her with a pretence of slow reluctance, and wonder whether his acting had done anything at all to win her back to his side.

It was still early, but there was nothing left to do except to retire to his own room. He lay back on the bed fully clothed and realized that he too needed to think. Now that he had reached Kyros he had to plan the last part of his mission; the death of Valedri and the recovery of the antidote. He also wanted to think about Antonella, the red-haired beauty resided here as Valedri's mistress, but from the way she had acted and yet apparently kept her own counsel, she did not appear to owe the man any great degree of loyalty. Who was she? And where did she really fit into the picture?

To most of the spinning questions in Larren's brain there was no answer, and several hours later he was still thinking hopelessly and getting no results. Then abruptly he heard a quiet tap at his door.

Larren tensed, wondering who could be calling upon him at this late hour of night. Then he got up and walked over to open the door.

Bruno stood there, still in his black tuxedo. The white-suited manservant who had served the dinner stood just behind him.

"I'm glad you're still up, Larren," Bruno said softly. "Mr. Valedri wants a quiet word with you."

Larren felt his stomach twist over. "At this time of night?" he asked.

Bruno smiled. "That's right. And let's make it quiet shall we? We don't want to disturb little Carla."

Larren knew then that Carla had not been able to win him any respite after all. Valedri had simply bided his time and waited until she was safely out of the way before taking any action.

Bruno stood on one side so that Larren could pass him and come out of the bedroom, and the hard look in the man's stony gaze showed that Larren

163

had no real choice in the matter. He walked slowly into the passageway and Bruno and his companion fell into step close behind him as he moved towards the top of the staircase.

His stomach was still twisting.

10

Deported

Larren expected to find Valedri waiting for him in the spacious lounge on the ground floor, but the room was empty and Bruno directed him through the dining-room and into the kitchen beyond. Here the silent manservant moved ahead to lead the way through yet another door and Larren found himself facing a flight of steep stone steps leading down into the vaults below the villa.

He knew that he was in a tight spot, but if there was any chance at all of getting out of it then that chance could only lay in continuing to act his part. He hesitated deliberately on the top step and turned to face Bruno.

"Why are we going down here?" he demanded as if puzzled.

Some thing that might have been the distorted shape of a smile flickered across

165

Bruno's face. "I thought I'd made that clear," he said softly. "We don't want to wake Carla from her slumbers."

With that Larren had to be satisfied, for it would have been obvious even to the dimmest tourist that Bruno was not inclined towards any further arguments or explanations. He shrugged his shoulders as though baffled and then turned again to follow the manservant down the steps. Bruno descended close behind him.

At the bottom of the steps Larren saw that the vaults were a maze of receding archways of red brick, some of the sections were stacked with junk and odds and ends, but mostly they were being used as wine cellars and were filled with large casks or racks of dusty bottles. For a cellar it was unusually clean and tidy, and it was well lit by naked electric light bulbs hanging from the ceiling between the arches.

Bruno gave Larren a nudge that started him walking again and they moved under the first arch across an empty floor of large flagstones. Beyond the next arch Larren saw his host waiting for him.

Valedri was standing by one of the racks and admiring the label on a dusty wine bottle. He looked up as they approached and calmly slipped the bottle back into its place. His dark face was expressionless, but there was a grim light of warning in his deep set eyes. He patted the dust from his hands and took a limping step forward as they halted before him.

"Ah, Mr. Simon Larren," he said flatly. "I'm sorry that I have so far proved to be a rather unattentive host, but I rather think that the time has come for us to get to know one another better."

Larren forced a smile. "By all means, but — " he looked helplessly around him — "why here?"

Valedri's face remained expressionless and his voice remained flat. "Just an old man's whim, Mr. Larren. You'll humour an old man surely?" His eyes glinted for a moment and then he went on. "Your left eye seems to have collected rather a nasty bruising somewhere in your recent travels — how did it happen?"

Larren felt his nerve ends jump as he remembered his beating from the man in

167

the big American Chevrolet, but nothing showed outwardly as he lied blandly. "It happened during the fighting when I rescued Carla. Savino almost knocked me out."

Valedri smiled thinly. "I should like to hear your version of that, my Carla sometimes has a tendency to exaggerate."

Larren looked uncomfortable. "I don't think Carla exaggerated," he said. He proceeded to tell the same story over again, re-phrasing Carla's words and including a few subtle alterations so that the tale did not sound too well rehearsed.

Valedri allowed him to finish and then asked grimly. "Is that all?"

"I think so. Why?"

"Because I don't believe it." Valedri's voice became hard and savage. "Let's stop playing cat and mouse, Larren. I might have enjoyed such games once but I'm an old man now and I don't have much patience left. At the moment I'm engaged in the biggest deal of my life and I half expected someone like you to come butting in. You may have fooled my daughter by hiring a few cheap hoodlums to pull a fake kidnap so that you could rush in firing blanks and do your heroic little 'here comes the cavalry' act — but you don't fool me."

Larren had not expected Valedri's suspicions to link him into an assumed partnership with Savino and he was almost as startled as he looked.

"That's ridiculous," he retorted. "And what about the man who was killed?"

Valedri said flatly. "There has been no report of the discovery of an unidentified body with two bullet holes in it, either in the Athens newspapers, or the radio news broadcasts. We have been watching both. I suggest that your actor friend probably cleaned off the ketchup, or whatever he used, and then walked away."

Larren said desperately, "The man was dead I tell you! But Savino was only unconscious, and then there was the other man who got away; they could have hidden the body. In fact it would be the logical thing for them to do."

"It could be plausible, Larren — but for one thing." Quite unexpectedly Valedri thrust his arm forward and viciously jabbed his index finger into the slight gash above Larren's left eye. "That cut betrays you," he screamed. His face was suddenly contorted and his controlled calm burst into trembling rage. "You're not only a liar, Larren, but a fool as well."

Larren jerked back as the sudden stab of pain flooded the whole of the left-hand side of his face. Immediately Bruno and his white-uniformed companion seized both his arms and gripped him firmly.

Larren managed to open his eyes again and said weakly, "I still don't understand what you mean."

"Don't you?" Valedri was showing the poisonous streak that had made him a top killer before the break-up of Murder Incorporated and a twenty-year prison sentence had held him down. "Then let me draw you a diagram. I recognized the possibility that someone like you might try to reach me through my daughter, so I had one of my best men watching every move she made. They found that man in an olive grove outside Athens early this morning with a broken neck." Valedri stopped to suck in a deep breath and then rasped on. "That man always wore a small ring on his right hand, Larren, a cheap gaudy thing with a sharp edge. The sort of ring that would leave a gash like the one above your eye if he had caught you with his fist — and the only clue that the police have is a trace of blood found on that ring."

Larren could feel the last of his hopes withering inside him as he struggled to find an answer. He said desperately, "Savino wore a ring. The fact that your man wore one as well is sheer coincidence."

Valedri shook his head. "I questioned Carla closely about that. Savino *never* wore a ring."

"Perhaps he didn't normally wear one, but he was wearing one last night." On the surface Larren was still defending himself, but deep down he knew that he was finished.

Valedri ignored his last protest and asked softly, "Who are you, Larren? Who are you working for?"

Larren made one last effort and shouted furiously. "My name *is* Larren, exactly as I told you, and I am not working for anybody. I don't know what the hell you're talking about and I think you must be bloody-well insane. You — " He broke off into a yelp of agony as the two men on either side of him deftly and viciously twisted his arms up behind his back. Then abruptly Bruno released him and spun him round so that the second man could seize both his arms. Then Bruno drove a clenched fist hard into his stomach.

Larren doubled up and hung there gasping. Bruno looked inquiringly at Valedri who simply nodded his head. For the first time in Larren's knowledge Bruno's hard face was lit up by a smile. The stony-eyed man reached into the pocket of his black tuxedo and drew out a short, solid length of rubber hose.

Larren knew he could probably break the grip of the man who held him, and with surprise on his side, plus his highly-specialized training he should be able to give a good account of himself even against the three of them. But if he tried he would still have to get clear of the island and that, with a hue and cry already raging, would be utterly impossible. It was night and the trip wires would be electrified and the guards would be patrolling with their killer dogs; and obviously the jetty and the motor launches would be well policed. His only hope was to wait until he could make an escape attempt without raising an alarm.

Bruno was obviously enjoying himself. He spat upon each of his palms in turn and rubbed them carefully upon the back of his fists as he swapped the length of hose from hand to hand. Then he slashed the weapon in a swift cutting stroke across Larren's ribs. He reversed the stroke in an expert back-hand blow and finished up with a neat downward chop that sent a wave of agony rushing through Larren's shoulder as it burst against his collar bone. Larren uttered a series of exclamations that were something between screaming and groaning and twisted helplessly against the man who held him.

Valedri said harshly, "I'll say it again, Larren. Who are you? And who are you working for?"

When Larren could answer he said hoarsely, "I don't — don't know what you mean."

Bruno set to work again. The rubber hose seemed to be slamming into Larren from all angles and each succeeding blow made him writhe and squirm. He was sobbing for breath and retching with the nausea of pain, and then one of Bruno's cutting blows landed close to his left hip which was already black and blue from the previous night and he fainted into the explosion of pure white agony.

When he came round he was choking and Valedri was pouring a bottle of sweet red wine over his face. He spluttered and was dragged back to his feet, still only semi-conscious.

Valedri said grimly, "I'm sorry, but we could not be bothered to run upstairs for water." He paused and demanded, "Are you ready to talk yet?"

"Can't talk. Don't know anything." Larren mumbled faintly.

Bruno drew back his length of rubber piping and struck again. Larren was experienced enough to know that the only possible course of action when unable to escape torture was to go unconscious as quickly and as often as possible, and without any concentration of effort whatever he promptly passed out again.

Valedri revived him with another bottle of wine, but he had no idea of how long the process lasted. When he was on his feet once more the ex-racketeer again asked his savage questions.

"Who is paying you, Larren? Who set up that phoney kidnap and rescue deal? It *was* a put-up job, wasn't it, Larren?"

Larren shook his head.

Bruno hit him and he found that fainting was now the easiest thing in the world.

* * *

The whole world was reeling round with a gentle swaying movement when Larren's senses finally stirred, and he groped his way reluctantly back to consciousness.

175

He did not want to awake and he tried vainly to fight off the increasing sense of awareness. Then slowly it penetrated into his dulled mind that this was a different awakening from the others; he was no longer lying on the cold flagstones of the cellar but upon something soft and yielding, and there was nobody pouring sweet wine over his face to revive him. With an effort he stopped fighting and allowed his senses to become clearer. Then he opened his eyes.

He was in the cabin of a large motor launch and lying comfortable in the single bunk. Through the only porthole he could see the moving blue of the Aegean and the grey-white sky of early dawn. Now that he was recovering he could both feel and hear the vibration of the launch's engine.

With the sharpening of his senses came the return of pain and it seemed that his whole body was just one merging mass of bruises, blending together in a thousand throbs and aches. His left hip was again stiff and immovable and he wondered whether he was capable of standing up and walking. He felt very sick and the sopping state of his shirtfront made him believe for a moment that he had already retched, but then he remembered again those conveniently-placed bottles that Valedri had emptied over him and realized that it was only wine.

Slowly his thoughts took shape and he began to wonder what they meant to do with him now. The fact that he was at sea provided one possible answer, and it seemed most likely that he was to be simply dropped over the side.

At the moment the thought did not disturb him for his brain was still foggy and he was unable to think straight. In fact it was several minutes before he noticed that he was not even tied up and that he was free to move around. However, before he could think any farther and take advantage of his freedom, the cabin door opened and Bruno ducked under the low deckhead.

Valedri's chief lieutenant no longer wore his smart tuxedo but had changed into faded jeans and an old sweat shirt, a more business-like rig-out for sailing. He stood with both hands on his hips and regarded Larren coldly with his stone-grey eyes.

Then he said flatly, "You're a lucky guy, Larren. Angelo is pretty sure that you're just another crummy crook trying to muscle in on our present business — but there is a small element of doubt, and for Carla's sake he's gone soft on killing you."

Bruno sounded slightly disgusted with his own words and went on. "In the old days Angelo would have cut your liver out for far less reason than he has to suspect you now, but he doesn't want to take a chance on upsetting the girl. She means a hell of a lot to him, and he's afraid of how she might react if you did prove to be on the level and she discovered that he had put a bullet in your guts."

He paused, but Larren was incapable of answering, so he began again. "But he still isn't taking any chances, Larren. He's sending you back to the mainland where you can't possibly interfere. We left Kyros while it was still dark and

Carla was sleeping, and she'll be told that you left of your own free will when you heard that I was making an early trip into Athens. She'll be mad that you didn't say goodbye, but Antonella will have a sympathetic woman-to-woman talk with her and convince her that you probably did come to the island for your own motives but that you were unable to face her after you chickened out."

Larren's brain was gathering speed, and that and instinct warned him that Bruno might be setting some kind of trap. Grimly he returned to the part he had adopted and snapped tartly.

"I still don't know what all this was about, but you most certainly haven't heard the last of it. As soon as I reach Athens I shall go straight to the police!"

Bruno laughed. "If you're the man we think you are you won't dare go near a police station, because they'll want proof of your cock-and-bull story too. And in the unlikely chance of that story being true you'll find that you'll have to explain more fully about the dead man you claim was left behind at that beach-front villa.

Your delay in reporting that will make things look bad for you, so either way you can only stir up more trouble for yourself. And Angelo pays you the compliment of believing that you have more sense than to do that."

Larren hoped that he looked as subdued and beaten as he felt.

Bruno turned to go and ended quietly. "We'll be reaching Athens in about an hour, and if you'll take my advice you'll catch the next plane back to England. Angelo may be giving you the benefit of the doubt, but if I ever see you again I'll probably kill you."

And with that parting gesture he went back on deck and slammed the cabin door behind him.

★ ★ ★

The sun had climbed higher above the eastern horizon and the sky had gradually changed to a pale, cloudless blue when Valedri's launch drew into Tourkolimano harbour at Athens. The glittering reflection from the pure azure

180

waters made Bruno screw up his eyes as he steered through the maze of small water craft; there were boats and yachts of all shapes and sizes, and even a magnificent, three-masted schooner with an ebony-black hull that lay gracefully near the harbour mouth. Bruno cut the throttle of the launch and drifted in to the quay between two more large motor boats. He had two of Valedri's men with him and he ordered one ashore to take the launch's mooring rope. The second man he sent to bring Larren up on deck.

A few moments later Larren stumbled out of the cabin and stood blinking in the strong sunlight. He looked around the harbour with its army of slanting masts and gleaming white hulls, and then his gaze turned towards Bruno.

Bruno said grimly, "As I said before, you're a very lucky man, Larren. Get going, and don't play with the big boys any more. They're too rough for you."

Larren killed the burning urge to send his fist smashing into that hard, taunting face and turned away towards the quay. Even if he had felt capable of another fight there were still three of them to contend with. It would be nothing short of madness to ask for another beating up.

* * *

A hundred yards away along the quay a tall, young-looking man with the slim, graceful figure of a ballet dancer sat at one of the pavement tables outside a small taverna. He was sipping slowly at a small cup of black, Turkish coffee, but he lowered the cup and a start of recognition flickered in his soft brown eyes as he observed Larren on the deck of the launch. He stared at the scene and noted the obvious signs of the beating that Larren had taken, and then he squinted his eyes to read the name on the launch's bow.

He recognized the boat as Angelo Valedri's and his face hardened as he watched Larren propelled ashore. He swore then, very foully and very angrily in precise, Oxford-accented English.

11

Back into the Storm

Larren called a taxi to take him back to the Hotel Sparta, and again he was almost goaded into violence when the driver promptly demanded his money in advance. He controlled himself with an effort and conceded sourly that the man had a perfect right to take such precautions with a passenger who looked as though he had just journeyed face first through a mincing machine. He paid up, but as he did so the expression in his grey-green eyes at least ensured him a conversation-free ride. The killer streak in Larren's make-up was showing very clearly in that moment, and even a man who could not recognize it could detect its hidden menace.

When he reached the hotel Larren went straight up to his room before any of the staff had the opportunity to notice or comment upon his appearance. He was glad now that he had paid two weeks' rent in advance to reserve the room before leaving, for although he had had to explain to the desk clerk that he might be absent for a few days he had been allowed to retain his key. Once in the room he made straight for the whisky bottle and poured a stiff shot into the nearest glass; then he drained it in one long slow movement and waited for the glow to hit his stomach. When it came he felt slightly better, and he poured himself another before sitting down on the bed. It was early for drinking, but right now he didn't give a damn what time of day it was.

For a few moments he simply sat there, incapable of doing anything except absorbing the luxury of the warming glow as the neat spirit circulated through his stomach. Then at last he threw back the second glass and reluctantly stood up. Wincing slightly he began to pull off his clothes and drop them on to the floor, his wine-sodden shirt he hurled angrily into the far corner. He stripped naked and then regarded his body grimly in the tall mirror inside the door of his wardrobe. It didn't look quite as bad as it felt, but it was still a very unpretty mess. He grimaced painfully as he touched the blue-black outline of his left hip bone, and then he turned and limped into the shower.

The hot water had a soothing effect that helped to ease the dull throbbing that nagged at every nerve and muscle in his body, but it also had the effect of washing away the small amount of energy that he still retained and left him feeling as weak as a kitten. He knew that cold water would revive him, but at the moment he did not want reviving and so he let the shower continue to run hot. When he finally came out he patted himself dry with tentative dabs of the big towel and then returned to the bedroom.

Still naked he crossed over to a large framed picture that hung against the wall and reached up to take it down. He laid it face down on the bed and his unsmiling mouth relaxed a little as he saw that his automatic and his sheath knife were still where he had left them, taped carefully to the back of the picture. The heavy, gilt frame was much thicker than the glass and the hardboard backing behind the picture, and that had enabled it to hang flat against the wall with Larren's armoury completely hidden. Larren removed both weapons and then replaced the picture on the wall.

Returning to the bedside he picked up the room service telephone, and when the desk clerk in the foyer answered he instructed that he was to be called at four p.m. He waited for the clerk to acknowledge the time and then rang off.

Wearily he dropped down on the bed, still naked but not bothering to crawl between the sheets. He placed both his automatic and his knife beneath the pillow within easy reach of his hand and then glanced at his watch. It was now eight fifteen and that gave him almost eight hours of sleep before he intended to do any thinking about his next move. He closed his eyes and was unconscious almost immediately.

* * *

As the first knock sounded on his door Larren's hand closed firmly over his automatic, then the knocking continued and he heard the lift boy calling his name. He relaxed and sat up slowly. It seemed impossible that eight hours could have passed so quickly, but a glance at his wrist-watch soon confirmed the fact and he got reluctantly to his feet. The lift boy called his name again and this time he answered.

There was a scratching movement at the foot of the door and then a folded newspaper appeared. In rehearsed, but clumsy, English the boy called out that this was the English paper and all part of the service. Larren thanked him and then heard his footsteps retreating down the corridor.

Larren was now feeling stiffer than ever and as he moved towards the shower he found that the limp in his left leg had become more pronounced. He entered the cubicle and turned the water fully on to cold, and flinched when the spray hit him. After a few moments he felt freshly invigorated and decided that he was almost fit to start living again.

He stayed under the shower for another ten to fifteen minutes and then carefully dried and dressed in clean slacks and an open-necked shirt. The bedroom was hot and stuffy even with the window open and he again decided to forego wearing a tie. His hip hurt as he stooped to tie his shoes but at last he was ready. He crossed to the door and felt another twinge from his hip as he bent down to pick up the newspaper.

The paper was a day old and headlined twenty-seven more victims to the red death; four had died in Italy, eight in France, and fifteen in Great Britain.

Larren stared at the headline without reading any further, and then slowly his fist clenched and crumpled the glaring black letters. He dropped the paper on the floor and turned to put on his jacket. Then he went back to the bed.

He took the automatic and the knife from under the pillow and slipped the gun into his right-hand jacket pocket;

the knife went into the inside pocket of his jacket and fitted into an undetectable sheath that hung inside the lining. That inside pocket was an unexpected place from which to produce a knife, and the hiding place would also fool an amateur searcher looking for the more conventional shoulder holster.

Larren felt far more capable now with the automatic lying heavy in his pocket and the slight weight of the knife against his breast; almost capable enough to completely ignore the aching bruises that covered his body. And that grim headline had told him exactly what his next move must now be.

He had wasted far too much time on the subtle approach and all he had received for his pains were two severe beatings that he had been forced to take to maintain his part. Well, he was acting a part no longer. He was Simon Larren, a trained killer and an expert with a knife, a gun, or his bare hands; and from now on he didn't give a damn who realized it. Too many people had died while he had fooled around in Carla Valedri's bed and now the time for winning confidences was past. His brief trip to Kyros had at least enabled him to size up the layout of the villa and the island's defences, and now he was going to take advantage of that knowledge. He was going to obtain a launch and make a quick silent murder raid under the cover of darkness, and anyone who got in his way was going to die.

Grimly he opened up his suitcase and took out a small, flat box that was roughly the size and shape of a cigar box. The contents of that box had been purchased before he left London and had been very difficult to obtain; but they were also very necessary, for they were the items that were going to make Angelo Valedri talk before he died. Larren slipped the box into his left-hand jacket pocket and then straightened his coat and left the hotel room. He went down to the hotel car park and found his hired Renault still standing where he had left it. Climbing in he started the engine and headed back to the small boat harbour where he had been pushed ashore that same morning.

There was a sharp glitter in his grey-green eyes as he drove through the fast Athens traffic.

★ ★ ★

As Larren drove away from the Hotel Sparta another car started up and began to follow him from a discreet distance. The second car was a large, imported Vauxhall and was also hired. Its driver was the tall, slim young man with the ballet-dancer figure who had watched as Larren had been forcibly ejected from Valedri's launch. His name was Adrian Cleyton, and his eyes, although a soft, almost effeminate, brown, were also hard and glittering. He made sure that Larren did not spot him as he kept the Renault in sight.

★ ★ ★

It was exactly four-thirty as Larren turned his car into the fast traffic stream that swirled round Omonia Square like a sea of ugly glass and chromium goldfish in

191

a waterless bowl. The shops that had been closed during the full heat of early afternoon were now raising their shutters, and the swarms of shoe shine boys and lottery ticket sellers were once more trying to drum up trade. The attendants in the little pavement kiosks that sold everything from postcards to shaving brushes and never seemed to close were again sitting up and paying attention. The dozing street-corner vendors who sat over their braziers of hot chestnuts or roasted corncobs were looking more alert as they scanned the thickening crowds for prospective customers, and the rich smell of roasting meat came from the large joints turning on the spits in the open doorways of the tavernas. Larren ignored it all as he speeded up the wide road past the Athens Academy and the University, and then nipped smartly through the traffic lights before the Parliament building at the top of Syntagma Square.

He turned again towards the sea some eight kilometres away, passing the now familiar sight of Hadrian's Arch and then the sixteen majestic columns of the Jupiter temple on his left. Again he barely noticed them as he drove by, for his thoughts left no room for any conscious admiration of either Athens or its ancient glory.

He simmered impatiently with every red light that caught him as he drove out of the city centre and it was another ten minutes before he finally saw the dancing blue of the Aegean ahead. He turned right on the Piraeus road and roared past the crowded beaches that faced the sea. A few minutes later he slowed down as the road curved inland to swing round the beautiful bay of Tourkolimano Harbour.

Larren eased his foot almost off the accelerator and drove very slowly as his gaze searched the jaunty miscellany of colourful boats with their sun-bleached decks and shining paint and brasswork. The berth where Valedri's launch had tied up that morning was empty, but Larren did not relax until he had assured himself that the boat had not merely moved to another part of the harbour. He felt that he would be quite happy to tangle with Bruno again at some future date, but right now he wanted to avoid any clash that might jeopardize the job at hand.

When he was fully satisfied that the launch was nowhere in sight he turned the Renault off the main road and drove a few yards down a side street where he felt that he could safely park. A Greek policeman watched him draw to a stop and something in the man's abrupt stare caused Larren to continue to watch him in his driving mirror. The policeman was frowning as he looked towards the car, and after a moment's hesitation he began to walk slowly towards it.

For a moment Larren failed to understand the reason behind the policeman's interest, and he wondered whether he was violating the parking laws. He was just about to pull away in case he was in a no parking area when a glimpse of his own reflection in the mirror provided the true answer. The battered state of his face was enough to make any policeman suspicious.

He swore angrily, for if he drove off

now it would make the man doubly suspicious, and as he had to return to the harbour to find a boat he might easily bump into the man again. The only safe course of action was to brazen the issue out, and that thought made him realize that the gun in his pocket made a somewhat large bulge. The last thing he could afford now was for the Greek police to become interested in his activities and reluctantly but swiftly he removed his armoury and the flat packet from his jacket pocket and slipped them under the driving seat out of sight. Then he got out of the car and carefully locked it behind him.

The Greek policeman stopped by his shoulder but Larren paused to pocket his car keys before turning round. He let an expression of surprise cross his face as though noticing the man for the first time.

The policeman said something curtly in Greek.

"I'm sorry," Larren apologized. "But I only speak English."

"You are English?" He sounded as

though he doubted the fact.

Larren assured him that he was English.

The policeman still looked doubtful. "Tourist?" he said at last.

For a moment Larren was afraid that his temper was about to explode as he realized that he was back to acting a part again, and he controlled himself with an effort that he was sure the man must notice as he answered. "That's right, I'm here on holiday."

The policeman's expression was still sharp and professional and he tapped his own eye meaningly. "You have an accident," he demanded.

Larren touched the bruised region of his own face and forced what he hoped was a rueful smile. "Your Greek wine is too strong. After six glasses I fell down and hit my face on the pavement."

The rueful smile must have been a success for it brought an answering smile in return. "You like our Greek wine, yes?"

Larren repeated his own smile and agreed amiably. "The wine is very good, but my head for it is poor."

The Greek laughed and then said abruptly. "Where you go now?"

Larren could see no gain in lying so he gestured to the harbour and admitted honestly. "I'm hoping to hire a boat that will take me out to sea." Then he added not so honestly. "I want to do some fishing."

The policeman looked towards the harbour and shrugged. "These are all private boats. Not for hire." He looked back again and repeated the shrug. "You can try. Perhaps someone will take you. I wish you luck."

Larren realized that the policeman was satisfied and that he was free to go, and after politely thanking the man for his help he walked away towards the harbour. The man stood by the Renault to watch him go so there was no opportunity for him to retrieve his automatic and knife. The fact that he was unarmed again irritated him, but there was no real reason why he should need a gun at this stage and after a few minutes he gave up worrying. He could re-arm himself after he had found a boat, for by then the policeman would probably be miles away.

He walked down to the harbour and then began to circle hopefully around the quay. He wanted a small launch but every craft he saw that would fit his requirements was unattended and he began to feel that perhaps he had come to the wrong place. These boats were all privately-owned pleasure craft and even if he could find one with the owner aboard the odds were very much against him being able to rent the boat for a night.

A fat man in flowered shorts and a panama hat was watching him from the aft deck of a small motor yacht and Larren decided that he had nothing to lose by making inquiries. He didn't want to hire the yacht but the man might tell him where he could hire a launch.

He moved closer to the edge of the quay and called out optimistically. "Excuse me, but do you speak English?"

The fat man's vague stare brightened. "Ah," he replied. "You speak English."

"Yes," Larren agreed patiently. "But

do you speak English?"

The fat man beamed and shook his head. "No, I don't speak English." Then he laughed delightedly.

Larren gave up and turned away.

He circled slowly round the harbour, stopping occasionally when he found a boat that was inhabited but failing to get any intelligent response. It seemed that nobody who owned a boat at Tourkolimano could speak English. Larren became gradually more exasperated and began to seriously consider the possibilities of simply climbing aboard one of the unattended launches and stealing it. At the same time he remembered that he had not eaten since the previous day and realized that he was extremely hungry.

He decided abruptly that he would snatch a quick meal at the nearest taverna and then continue his search on a full stomach and in a better frame of mind. He could not take a boat out to Kyros until after dark anyway, so there was no immediate hurry. He turned sharply away from the harbour and almost walked straight into a slim, black-haired youth in jeans and an open red shirt who had been edging up behind him.

The youth stepped back quickly and gave him an unsavoury grin that twisted up one corner of his mouth. "You speak English?" he asked.

Larren was becoming weary of that constant query and he simply nodded his head.

The youth came a step nearer and lowered his voice. "You English tourist? I speak English too." His voice dropped even lower as he added. "You looking for pretty girl perhaps?"

Larren resisted the temptation to throw him in the harbour and said shortly, "No." Then he pushed past and moved on.

The pimp caught at his arm. "What you want then? Anything you want I can fix. Anything."

Larren closed one hand over the fist that had locked on his coat sleeve and twisted it away. The youth yelped and wriggled and Larren suddenly felt too disgusted to even hit him. He pushed the hand away from his coat and let it go.

The pimp looked up at him hopefully. "Anything," he repeated and there was a pathetic cringe to his voice.

Larren hesitated. Then he said slowly. "What about a boat? Can you find someone who will hire me a launch for the night?"

The youth blinked. "A boat," he objected doubtfully. "Why you want a boat?"

Larren turned away but the youth called after him eagerly. "Wait. I know a man who will hire you a boat."

Larren turned back. "All right," he ordered. "Show me where." He understood the smiling change in the boy's manner and added curtly, "Payment is only on delivery."

The smile faded, but instantly picked up again, "Okay, I show you." He turned and gestured to Larren to follow him along the quay. Larren fell into step behind him.

After a few yards the youth glanced up again, hesitated, and then said softly, "I have some good pictures — you want to see?"

Larren said nothing.

"Very good pictures," he insisted. "A man and a woman together. The woman is — "

Larren said flatly, "Just show me the boat."

The youth scowled and relapsed into sulky silence. Then, fifty yards farther along the quay, he stopped and pointed at a sleek black motor launch. "There. The owner is in the cabin."

He waited sullenly while Larren dropped a 100 drachma note into his hand, and seemed unsure whether he ought to demand more. Larren didn't wait for him to make up his mind but turned to board the launch.

The launch was moored close to the harbour wall and he was able to drop down lightly on to the well-scrubbed deck. The boat appeared to be deserted, but a glance back at his guide showed that the youth was not running away but still stood there watching him, so it seemed unlikely that he had been duped. He saw that the cabin door was open and ducked his head to pass inside.

Two men were waiting for him in the gloom. One was the man named Dimitri who owned the beach villa where Carla Valedri had been kidnapped; and the other was a tall, blue-jawed Greek with brittle eyes and a slim moustache. Both men held automatics.

Instinctively Larren knew that the tall, dangerous-looking Greek was the mysterious Christos with whom he had tangled at the villa. He recalled the old saying that it never rains but it pours, and decided that he was back into the storm with a vengeance.

12

Brothers in Blood

Larren stood with his head still bowed to get under the low deckhead of the launch's cabin and tasted the bitter bile of frustration rising in his throat. His hands tightened in cold, helpless fury as he gripped the two sides of the door frame and the blood drained from his knuckles until they shone like white ivory. His thoughts swirled in a pool of hatred as he silently cursed the suspicious policeman who had caused him to part from his knife and gun, and he could quite happily have taken the pimp who had steered him into this trap and throttled the life from his grubby body.

The tall, blue-jawed Greek said quietly, "Won't you step inside, Mr. Larren?" Then he added, "I take it that you are Mr. Simon Larren?"

With the two squat-nosed automatics

pointing directly at his stomach Larren had no choice other than to accept the invitation. He stepped down into the cabin and straightened his shoulders. His hands he kept well away from his sides with the palms facing outwards. He swallowed his rage and said harshly, "That's right — and you must be Christos."

The Greek bowed slightly without moving either his eyes or his gun. "That is correct." Again the gun and eyes remained steady as he gestured to the man beside him with his free hand. "I believe you have already met Dimitri."

Dimitri was smirking broadly and the wrinkled line of the black moustache on his upper lip gave his face an almost comic look, but his manner had changed now that he had a gun in his hand and Larren found it hard to picture him as the amiable little host from the beach party.

He said flatly, "Yes, we have met."

There was the sound of footsteps on the deck outside and for a moment Larren felt a flicker of hope. Then he realized that it could only be the pimp and the flicker died.

Christos snapped curtly. "Stay outside, Nico. Mr. Larren might be tempted into playing tricks if the cabin becomes too crowded, and I should hate to find that you had been pushed in my way and shot by mistake."

The youth mumbled an answer in Greek, he sounded sulky again but he remained just outside the doorway as ordered.

Christos reached into his jacket pocket with his free hand and drew out a small roll of notes. He tossed them casually past Larren and through the door. "Pick them up, Nico. Then slide the cabin door shut and go back to your own business. We will not need you again."

Larren heard the scuffling sound as the youth grabbed at his money, then the cabin door slammed into place behind him with a slight bang. The muffled footsteps of the departing pimp faded and ceased as he left the launch.

Christos said calmly, "A distasteful little person, but he does have his useful moments. It was he who informed me that you had been deported from Kyros. I pay him to keep an eye on the arrivals and departures of Valedri's launch. His description of you fitted the Simon Larren who had gate-crashed Dimitri's party so I guessed that you must be the same man. I also reasoned that as you had obviously not been able to win Valedri's confidence as expertly as you won Carla's you would eventually come searching for some other means of returning to the island. So I decided to spend the rest of the day on my launch and wait for you, having first instructed Nico to warn me as soon as you came snooping around." He paused there and smiled softly. "I must admit, Mr. Larren, that you made me sweat a little during our encounter at the villa. I realized then that you are not the sort of man to give up your assignment, whatever it may be; and as your activities appear to endanger mine it was clear that something must be done about it."

Larren found that his first reaction of fury had passed and he was able to speak calmly as he answered.

"I think the honours were even at the

villa, I sweated a little myself."

Christos smiled. "You are an excellent operative, Larren. I did not think that anyone could out-wait me in the darkness as you did. I believe you were also out on the dunes before you entered the house, were you not?"

Larren nodded.

"I thought so. I sensed it, but it is so long since I have experienced such sensations that I thought my instincts were playing me tricks."

Larren said quietly, "You're a war veteran, obviously."

Christos nodded. "I spent the war years with the Greek resistance movement and carried the acting rank of Colonel. Dimitri was my chief lieutenant then, and my brother Savino was just a fire-eating boy with more courage than sense. By day we drank wine and made love to the peasant girls in the mountains, and by night we blew up trains and sabotaged practically everything we could lay our hands on, from telephone poles to petrol dumps. I learned to kill German sentries by stealth and a quick thrust of a knife.

I enjoyed it and I was very sorry when the war ended. Life has been somewhat dull ever since."

The tall Greek's tone had mellowed as his memories carried him back into the past, but his caution had not relaxed. His eyes were a very light blue, and again Larren thought that brittle was the only word to describe them, they looked hard enough to splinter and shatter at the slightest touch. He now knew without doubt that his instinct had been right about Christos at the villa, this man had been cast from the same mould as his own, and was probably the most dangerous adversary that he would ever meet.

His thoughts were interrupted as Christos regarded him levelly and inquired. "And you, Larren? Where did you learn to move like a cat in the night?"

Larren knew that there was nothing to be gained in lying to this man. Instinct had helped him to recognize Christos as a killer of his own kind, and undoubtedly that same instinct would have served the other man in turn. Calmly he said:

209

"I made two parachute drops into occupied Holland and worked with the resistance there. The same sort of job as yours, but without the wine and the peasant girls."

Christos smiled, his moustache, unlike Dimitri's, was a very slim pencil line, and that plus his crinkly black hair and very white teeth made him a handsome man in a deadly, mature way. His blue jaw and dark skin meant nothing when he smiled.

He said softly, "I could have guessed as much. I think we have a lot in common, Mr. Larren, and I should like to continue this conversation; but I shall also feel much more sure of myself when normal safety precautions have been taken and your hands are securely tied." His tone changed and he said curtly, "Dimitri!"

Dimitri knew exactly what he had to do. He produced a length of cord that was already looped into a noose and moved a pace forward. "Turn around, Larren," he ordered.

"Keep your hands well away from your sides as they are now until you have your back to me, then bring your hands together behind you."

Larren did exactly as he was told.

He heard Dimitri step closer behind him and knew that the man must now be standing in Christos's line of fire. His heart began to race unevenly as he realized that once he was safely trussed up he was as good as dead, and that any attempt to escape must be made now. The odds against success were pitifully thin, but after his hands were tied they would be thinner still.

He felt the noose scrape along the backs of his hands and then tighten around his wrists as Dimitri manipulated it with one hand. The man coiled the cord twice more and then there was a moment's pause. Larren knew that Dimitri would be slipping his automatic into his pocket now that his prisoner was half secured, for he would need both hands to tie the final knots. He waited until he felt his captor pulling on the cords again with both hands, and then he acted just as the final knots were about to be tied, hurling himself backwards and thrusting his feet hard against the bulkhead to give himself extra momentum.

Dimitri made a harsh gasping sound as Larren's shoulders slammed into his chest, and the impact sent him half falling and half staggering across the cabin. In that confined space Larren's falling body struck Dimitri again about the knees and this time he collided with Christos and then crashed to the floor. His gun was half-way out of his pocket again and the weapon skidded across the deck.

Larren was tearing his hands out of the entanglement of the loose cord as he fell and he had one hand free as his back met the wooden deck-boards with a resounding crash. In one desperate, wriggling movement he had scrambled over on to his knees and he saw Dimitri's automatic where it had fallen only a few feet away. He lunged towards it, but even as his hand closed over the butt a nailed boot stamped viciously at his fingers. He yelled with the fierce biting pain as the nails raked across his knuckles and was forced to release his grip. The automatic lay beneath his splayed-out fingers and the heavy boot was still grinding down on the back of his hand when he felt the cold snout of a second automatic jabbing hard into the side of his neck.

Larren knew that he had failed and remained absolutely still.

Christos said admiringly, "I expected that, Larren. But even so it almost took me by surprise. You're very fast."

Larren didn't answer. The Greek's boot was crushing his hand and he could see trickles of blood tracing a very fine network of red down his wrist. He heard Dimitri get up and was relieved when the man retrieved his automatic and Christos removed his boot.

Dimitri said savagely, "Let's try again, Larren." And he deliberately thrust one foot hard into the small of Larren's back to flatten him to the floor. Christos straightened up and stepped away, and Larren made no further attempts at resistance as Dimitri completed the job of lashing his wrists together.

Finally Christos said, "I think his movements will be suitably restricted now, Dimitri. Perhaps you will return on deck and take the launch out into the Aegean where we can be undisturbed, while I continue to entertain our guest."

Dimitri nodded without argument and Larren heard the cabin door slide open and then slam shut as the man went out.

There was a creak from the single bunk as Christos sat down, and then the tall Greek said, "Please turn round, Mr. Larren. I can hardly continue our conversation with the back of your neck."

Larren was glad to accept the invitation, for he was finding it both uncomfortable and undignified to sprawl face down on the floor. He twisted over on to his back, but as his bruised hands were then behind him and taking most of his weight he wriggled cautiously up to a sitting position and propped his shoulders against the bulkhead.

Christos watched him. "I would have helped you to sit up," he apologized. "But you will appreciate as well as I do that even a man with his hands tied can deliver a nasty kick in the crotch, and

214

I prefer to avoid the risk of any further unpleasantness."

"A logical precaution," Larren agreed. His hand was smarting badly but even so he found it hard to hold any malice towards this man.

Christos had relaxed a little now and he allowed the hand holding the automatic to rest on one knee. He said conversationally, "I believe we were reminiscing about the war years before that little interruption, were we not. I was saying that I found life rather dull. Of course I tried to inject it with some of the old pace and excitement; I spent several years running contraband in and out of Tangier, then I sold guns and explosives in the Middle East, and now I run a small crime syndicate here in Athens: but I still cannot quite reproduce the old conditions. In the resistance we were just a small handful of men fighting the full onslaught of Nazism, facing odds that seemed hopeless and living only to kill and maim as many of those jack-booted murderers as we could reach before we died. Now there is no such challenge left, and even though I have killed two or three times in the past years there is not the same amount of satisfaction. When you have to crawl a hundred yards through the mud on your belly with a knife in your teeth and soot on your face, and every moment expecting a rifle bullet to come tearing through your brain; and when your enemy is a fully-trained, well-armed, steel-helmeted soldier who must die in absolute silence to avoid raising the alarm; then there is satisfaction in killing. The execution of a double-crossing sneak thief in a Tangier warehouse becomes sordid by comparison."

Christos became silent, and for a moment both men gazed vacantly into each other's eyes. Larren could understand the note of regret in Christos's tone only too well, for he had killed his first man in exactly the way that Christos had described. Before he could answer, however, the launch's engine began to throb as Dimitri pulled the starter.

Christos came out of his reverie and demanded abruptly, "What about you,

Larren? Are you still working for one of the Intelligence departments of your country? or have you also turned to Lady Fortune and the rewards of crime?"

Larren smiled. "I've turned soft, I live on rich young widows and rich men's daughters."

"Like Carla Valedri?"

"That's right."

The launch began to move slowly out of the harbour as Christos said softly, "A pansy gigolo wouldn't have butted his head into that party at the villa for a millionaire's daughter, much less for a sex-happy nympho who's liable to flit straight on to the next hairy he-man who flexes his muscles and mentions the simple word 'bed'." He sounded annoyed, as though he had expected Larren to be perfectly frank. He went on in the same tone. "Who are you working for, Larren?"

The launch was gathering speed now and Larren judged that they must be leaving the harbour. He looked up at Christos and realized again that there was no real point in lying to this man.

Without changing his expression he said, "I'm strictly solo."

Christos grimaced. "It looks as though I shall have to accept your word on that. When you first walked into this cabin I meant to find out exactly who you are and what you are doing, and I assumed that I could make you talk. Now I can see from your face that Angelo Valedri has already tried that, and the fact that he released you can only mean that he failed to break your cover story. I am in a slightly better position than he was because I know for a fact that you are not the harmless gigolo you claim to be, but even so I doubt if I could succeed where Valedri has failed. In any case, it does not really matter whether you are working for yourself, or as an agent of British Intelligence, either way I cannot allow you to live."

Larren felt his stomach begin to move with a slow, sickening motion that had nothing to do with the bouncing of the launch as it roared at full throttle into the open sea. He said nothing.

Christos's face wrinkled into another

218

grimace that expressed a slight feeling of distaste. "I am really sorry, Larren. As I have said, there is no satisfaction in killing a helpless man, and I would have felt much happier if I had been able to kill you at the villa; but unfortunately I am playing for very high stakes, and you are simply too dangerous for me to take any chances." There was a note of genuine regret in his tone as he went on. "You and I are brothers, Larren, brothers by blood if not by birth, and your death will perhaps be the only one with which I shall ever reproach myself. This way I shall never know whether or not I could have out-witted you on equal terms in the darkness."

Larren said evenly, "It was a pity that your fat friend had to move; I should also like to know which one of us would have cracked first." He paused and then added, "What did happen to the body? The fact that it was not reported washed up on the beach somewhere was one of the reasons why Valedri refused to believe my story. He thought that I was in partnership with Savino, and that the whole thing was a piece of pure play-acting put on to fool Carla."

Christos shrugged. "We buried the body on the dunes. When I left the villa I merely drove the car out of hearing range in order to fool you into thinking I had been scared clean away, and then I doubled back to the beach where Dimitri was waiting for the launch that was to remove Carla. We warned the launch off and then returned together to deal with you, only by that time you had already escaped with Carla. We revived Savino and the other sentry whom you had knocked unconscious, and then, as nobody appeared to have heard the shooting, we decided that it would be best to conceal the body and cover the whole thing up. So far the Athens police have no idea that we exist, and I was anxious to keep it that way."

Larren felt strangely pleased that his judgement had been right at the villa, for he had guessed that either a boat or some other form of transport had been expected to take Carla away, but it was poor compensation for his present position.

Christos grinned suddenly and said, "By the way, my brother Savino is very annoyed with you; the wound in his arm is slight and means nothing, but his pride is badly damaged and Savino is a very vain young man."

It was Larren's turn to shrug. "It hardly matters now, does it?"

Christos nodded. "As you say, it hardly matters."

He stood up and crossed the small cabin to glance through the porthole, he steadied himself with his free hand as he moved and he was careful to keep out of the range of Larren's unbound feet. After a minute he turned back and said, "We are now several miles out to sea, and I think that's far enough." He slid back the cabin door and shouted up to Dimitri to stop the launch. The engines died and the boat gradually lost speed in a series of bouncing slaps as it skimmed over the waves. Soon it was rolling gently on the slight swell.

Christos turned back to face Larren. He made an expressive gesture with his shoulders and hands and said sadly, "I

221

wish we could have settled it at the villa."

Larren said quietly, "Perhaps we could do a deal. I'm not interested in any money that might be made from the Ameytheline antidote, I just want to see it put to use."

"So you are after the antidote, I knew it had to be that. I appreciate your motives, Larren, but unfortunately there are complications that do not concern the matters of personal profit. I am afraid that our motives would still be in opposition."

Larren accepted Christos's words with a shrug. He had not really expected any other answer, but it was a possibility that had to be tried.

Christos raised his automatic and said reluctantly, "Turn your head away from me, Larren. I'll make it quick and clean as a token of my respect. That's all I can do."

For a moment Larren's grey-green eyes gazed straight into the Greek's face, and he saw that Christos's eyes had again taken on that strange brittle look. Slowly he turned his head away. He had often heard that in the last few seconds before death the whole of a man's life would flash before him, but he knew now that this was wrong. He saw nothing but one single face from the past; the face of Andrea, the woman he had once loved and married. He saw her quite clearly as he waited for the single bullet from Christos's automatic to smash into the back of his head.

13

Andromavitch has Vanished

Dimitri was standing with his feet well apart to maintain his balance on the gently rolling launch, and his hands were clenched tightly on the wheel as he stared towards the heat-blurred hills that cradled Athens on the horizon. His eyes were narrowed against the combined dazzle of blue seas and skies, and the breaking swallow tails of foam that danced on every wave rendered him almost blind. His mouth was grim and he was wishing that Christos would get on with the job in the cabin, for although he had been a party to murder before he did not particularly enjoy it.

His mind went back to the gate-crashing incident when Larren had duped him into offering an invitation to join the beach party at the villa, and he swore bitterly. If only he had not been so keen to play his part of the cheerful host he would never have made that mistake, and then the course of events might not have necessitated this distasteful execution.

He heard Christos order Larren to turn his head and waited grimly for the single shot. And in the same moment he heard the fast approaching engine of a second launch.

He saw the boat immediately, still over half a mile away and almost hidden behind the twin, parting curtains of spray and foam that leapt up from its surging bows. It was bearing straight down upon the stationary launch and looming closer with every second.

Dimitri swore and shouted for Christos. The name was barked so sharply that for a moment Larren thought that Christos had actually fired, his body stiffened and his face twisted with expected anguish, and when he realized that he was still alive he was drenched with sweat and nearly retched. He heard Christos spin round and scramble swiftly out of the small cabin, but for the next few seconds his reactions left him as helpless as he would have been if that awaited bullet had actually torn his head apart.

When he was at last able to turn his head the cabin was empty, but through the open door he could see the legs of both Greeks as they stared towards the oncoming launch.

Dimitri uttered an angry exclamation in Greek and in the same instant Christos came scrambling back into the cabin as fast as he had left it.

He said harshly, "It's a police launch, Larren, and it's coming straight for us. What do you know about it?"

Larren found his voice and said hoarsely, "Nothing."

Christos still had his automatic in his hand, and in that moment Larren thought that his brief reprieve had run out. The tall Greek's brittle eyes had gone cold with fury and he seemed to waver on the point of pulling the trigger. Then abruptly he thrust the automatic into his pocket and pulled out a clasp knife. Larren flinched as the Greek snapped open the blade, and then Christos swiftly knelt beside him and slashed through the ropes that bound his hands.

Larren still did not understand as he struggled to stand up. Christos helped him and for a moment they stood face to face.

Christos had controlled that single flash of rage and now he spoke again with professional calm.

"It looks like your lucky day, Larren. I don't know what they want, but I do know that I can't afford to be caught with a corpse, or even a live prisoner, and that means that you and I must make a temporary truce. I know that you have no more wish than I have to become involved with the police, so I feel that I can trust you to remain silent when they arrive. To them, you will be my willing guest on a pleasure cruise, and neither of us can gain from letting them suspect otherwise." He smiled suddenly and finished, "In a way I am almost glad, Larren. This way we can start from scratch and attempt to kill each other in a more gentlemanly way. I still want to kill you, Larren, but if it becomes possible I should prefer to do it upon even terms."

Larren's wits were functioning normally now and he answered in the same tone. "I'll accept that. I'll help you to satisfy the police, providing you grant me a safe return to Athens.

"Agreed. And as I have no doubt that you will continue to get in my way I shall kill you the next time we meet."

The confident sound of that final promise made Larren shiver, but before he could answer they heard a new voice, slightly distorted by distance and again in Greek, and they knew that they were being hailed from the police launch through a loud-speaker.

Christos said quickly, "Those ropes!" He snatched up the severed cords that had secured Larren's wrists and thrust them through the open porthole that was on the blind side of the police launch. He hesitated for a moment, and then pulled out his gun and jettisoned that too. On deck Dimitri was answering the man with the loud-speaker.

Larren followed Christos up on deck

and saw that the launch was now only thirty yards away and swinging round in a slow curve to close the gap.

Christos rapped softly. "Dimitri, get rid of your gun. If they've got cause to stop us then they are sure to search us — and firearms will need explaining."

Dimitri obeyed without question, ducking swiftly into the cabin and dropping his automatic through the porthole. He rejoined them almost immediately and they watched in silence as the launch came alongside. Larren felt a grudging sense of admiration for the quick thinking and calm action of the tall Greek, and he knew the police could now strip both the launch and its occupants without finding any kind of incriminating evidence.

The two boats touched together with a gentle bump as the man at the wheel of the police launch brought her to an expert halt. A party of three policemen immediately jumped aboard the stationary launch and one of them pushed quickly past Christos's shoulder to the launch's cabin. He held his revolver at the ready and so did the second man, a sergeant who covered the three men on deck. The third member of the boarding party was a uniformed Inspector who still held his cone-shaped loud-speaker loosely by his side. On the deck of the launch that they had just left a very slim young man in the casual clothes of an English tourist stood watching the proceedings.

The slim man was a complete stranger to Larren, but he was definitely the odd man out among the uniforms of the Greek police and so attracted his immediate attention. He did not know that this was the man who had watched the latter stages of his deportation from Kyros at Tourkolimano, or that the man had since been trailing him through the streets of Athens. And, therefore, he was genuinely startled when the man thrust an accusing arm in his direction and cried dramatically in English.

"That's him, Inspector! That's the man!"

The Greek police Inspector stared hard at Larren and then turned back to the man on the other launch. He also spoke in English and there was both anger and suspicion in his tone as he rasped harshly, "This is not Loukas."

The man on the police launch waved his hands excitedly. "No, no, of course not. But this is the man whom I saw talking to Loukas just before the launch sailed."

The Inspector snapped a question in Greek to the policeman who had rushed into the launch's cabin, but obviously received a negative reply. The policeman came up on deck again, shrugged, and then stood to one side.

Christos decided it was time he spoke up and demanded curtly, "What is the meaning of this, Inspector? Why have you boarded my launch?"

The Inspector's face was dark and lean beneath his peaked cap, and there was an uncertain hesitancy in his tone, as though he suspected that he might eventually be called upon to apologize for his actions. He said slowly, "I regret the intrusion, sir, but my name is Kravakos, and I am an Inspector of the Athens police, and I have reason to believe that a wanted criminal named Loukas may be, or have been, aboard your boat."

"That's ridiculous," Christos exploded angrily. "You can't possibly be serious." He looked around as though expecting someone to assure him of this, and again Larren had to admire the way the Greek was handling the situation. Christos went on. "Surely you can see for yourself that myself and my two friends are the only persons on board."

"True," Kravakos admitted. "But even so, my informant claims that he saw Loukas come aboard this boat — and in the company of this man." He spoke the last sentence sharply and looked directly at Larren.

Larren said firmly, "I have never seen your informant before, and I have never heard of anyone named Loukas. I have absolutely no idea of what any of you are talking about."

"But I saw — "

"Silence!" Kravakos roared the one word savagely and effectively rendered the slim young Englishman speechless. He turned back to Larren and said harshly, "Peter Loukas is a criminal wanted for both bank robbery and murder; he broke into the Excelsior Exchange bank of Thessaloniki and killed a bank clerk while escaping. His picture has been circulated in every paper in Greece, and this gentleman, who is Mr. Adrian Cleyton, claims that he recognized Loukas from this picture when he saw him talking with you."

Larren looked from Kravakos to the man who called himself Adrian Cleyton, and then looked back again. "He's either blind, mistaken, or lying," he said flatly.

"That is so," Christos interrupted vehemently. "Mr. Larren is a friend of mine and I can vouch for him."

The man named Cleyton said tartly, "I am not lying, Inspector. I definitely saw your wanted man talking to this fellow Larren at the harbour just over half an hour ago. They both came aboard this launch."

"Then where is Loukas now?" Kravakos was almost snarling.

Cleyton shrugged. "I only know what I saw; for all I know he may have left the boat again while I was hunting for your policeman."

Kravakos swung back to Larren. "You, what is your name? And what are you doing in Greece?"

Larren said calmly, "My name is Simon Larren, and I am here on a short holiday."

"Your passport please." Kravakos held out his hand.

Fortunately Larren had his passport with him. It was made out in his own name, but had been provided by Smith several years ago and described his occupation as a travelling representative. He handed it over to the Greek Inspector who glared at it but did not return it.

Instead Kravakos turned to Christos. "And you, sir, your name please?"

"Christos. I am an Athens businessman. I also own this launch. This is my friend and secretary Dimitri."

Kravakos ignored Dimitri and demanded, "How long have you known Mr. Larren?"

Christos hesitated. "Well, about three hours actually." He spoke doubtfully as though he was just beginning to realize that perhaps he couldn't vouch for Larren so thoroughly after all. He continued. "We met over lunch in a taverna near Tourkolimano and discovered that we both shared similar memories from the war. So we talked, and drank retzina, and finally became friends. I then invited him to a short cruise on my launch."

"So! You have only known him for three hours?"

Christos looked uncomfortable and nodded.

Larren realized that unless he did something to avert it the cunning Greek was going to wriggle deftly out of their predicament while still leaving him firmly under suspicion. It would suit Christos perfectly, for he would be held in a Greek jail while Kravakos made further inquiries, while Christos could go ahead with whatever plans he had for obtaining the Ameytheline antidote from Valedri.

Quickly Larren said, "But you and I were together for the whole of those three hours, my friend. You know that I could not have been seen talking alone to any criminal during that time as this

Mr. Cleyton suggests."

Christos was caught, for he could not deny his own story now without an argument that might cause Kravakos to think that he, as well as Larren, might have something to hide. He smiled, as though delighted that the point had been made, and even Larren found it hard to believe that he was probably fuming underneath.

"That's right, Simon, we were together all the time."

It was the first time that he had ever used Larren's christian name, but he slipped it in convincingly as though they had been life long friends.

The hapless Kravakos quite obviously didn't know which story to believe, and the fact that his men were both watching him expectantly and waiting for him to decide failed to improve his temper. He glared at every suspect in turn and then snapped abruptly. "I am sorry, but I am not satisfied with all this. I must ask you three gentlemen to step aboard the police launch and accompany me back to Athens. One of my men will take this launch back into harbour for you."

Christos said angrily, "I refuse. You cannot treat my friends and myself like this just because this fool has made a mistake in identity."

The slim man looked indignant and snapped back. "I tell you there has been no mistake."

"The police station," Kravakos said with grim finality. "We will discuss the matter thoroughly at the police station."

Christos made a pretence of trying to outstare the Inspector, and then admitted defeat and stepped stiffly aboard the police launch. Larren and Dimitri followed him slowly.

A few moments later they were speeding back to Athens once more, with Christos's launch bouncing in their wake. Kravakos had refused to allow any further discussion or argument and so Larren stood in silence and watched the city and the Acropolis become clearer as they neared the mainland. Quite abruptly he realized that he might never have seen this view again, and without the arrival of Cleyton and the police he would by

237

now have been nothing more than a lifeless slab of weighted fish food on the sea bed of the Aegean. He began to wonder exactly what sort of game the slim young man named Cleyton was playing, but at that moment the answers did not appear to be as important as they would have been at any other time. The one solid fact among all the new complications was that Cleyton, whether deliberately or unwittingly, had saved his life, and even though he was now on his uncomprehending way to a Greek jail, Larren was very grateful just to be alive.

★ ★ ★

The police launch was fitted with radio so Kravakos was able to call two large black police cars and have them waiting at the harbour when they landed. He ordered Christos and Larren into the first one and rode with them to the police station; Dimitri and Cleyton followed in the second car in the care of a sergeant. When they arrived they were separated, as Larren had expected, and he found himself waiting in a small bare room adjoining Kravakos's office under the watching eye of a uniformed policeman. His guard spoke only Greek so conversation was impossible, but Larren guessed that Kravakos would be interrogating the others one by one and checking on their stories.

There was nothing he could do except wait and wonder. He didn't doubt that Christos and Dimitri would be able to clear themselves, but he had a horrible feeling that proving his own innocence might not be so easy. For although Christos undoubtedly had friends to whom he could appeal, and probably even a lawyer on hand, there was no one in Athens on whom Larren could call for a reference of character.

For over an hour and a half Larren was forced to sit alone in the small room with only the silent guard for company. He spent the time in a vain attempt to reason out why the mysterious stranger named Cleyton should have made his blandly lying accusations, but he could still find no answers. The only conclusions he could reach were that Cleyton had been either deliberately acting to save his life, or that the man was attempting to get him jailed out of the way and had saved him by accident. And as both possibilities were still full of whys and hows his reasoning did not take him much farther. He had to admit that he was baffled and leave it at that.

He was still brooding over the maze of question marks when Kravakos finally sent his sergeant to fetch him. Larren followed the man down a short corridor and into a small office where Kravakos sat behind a square desk. The Greek Inspector had removed his jacket and peaked cap and sat with his tie loosened and the top button of his shirt undone. His swarthy face was showing signs of weariness and a slackly-reined temper, and Larren guessed that he had already questioned the other three thoroughly without making progress.

Kravakos offered him a seat and Larren sat down. He said shortly, "I hope your inquiries have satisfied you, because I'm sorry to say that I'm already tired of your hospitality."

Kravakos looked as though he was forcing himself to count ten silently before answering, then he said tiredly, "Mr. Larren, I am sorry, but this man Peter Loukas is a wanted murderer; and it is my job to follow every lead that might enable me to catch him. Now Mr. Cleyton has made a definite statement that he saw you talking to Loukas before boarding Mr. Christos's boat. Mr. Christos has also made a statement to the effect that you were in his company for most of the three hours previous to accepting his invitation to join him on a short cruise. But note, Mr. Christos can only swear to most of that time. There was one short gap just before sailing when he left you to get some cigarettes at a taverna. Just a brief few minutes, but still time for you to have been seen talking to Loukas as Mr. Cleyton describes. Mr. Christos does not think it very probable for the time was too short, but he admits that it is just possible."

Kravakos stopped there, and Larren saw how neatly Christos had twisted things to his advantage, but it was no more than he had expected.

Kravakos went on. "On the face of it I am inclined to believe your story, Mr. Larren, for although I have had that area covered from the moment Mr. Cleyton made his accusations, there has been no report of Loukas being seen in the area. The only real cause for doubt is that I cannot think of any possible motive for Mr. Cleyton to lie." He paused, and then added softly, "Can you?"

Larren shook his head. "I think I told you, I've never seen him before in my life."

Kravakos seemed to accept that. Then he suddenly snapped, "What happened to your face, Larren? Where did you get those bruises?"

Larren flinched at the unexpected ferocity of Kravakos's tone and answered. "It was through drinking, I had a bit too much and fell down a flight of stone steps." As he spoke he prayed that Kravakos would not become really suspicious and insist that he remove his shirt, for the multiple bruises that covered the rest of his body could never be explained by a simple fall.

Kravakos relaxed a little and sat back. He said slowly, "I'm going to have to hold you while I make a few more inquiries, Mr. Larren."

Larren looked shocked. "You can't hold me here without a reason."

"No, but I can hold you for a short time on suspicion. If you prove to be innocent I shall apologize, but until then I cannot take a chance and let you go."

"What about Christos and Dimitri?"

"I have already released them. Mr. Christos's brother, a man named Savino, arrived with a lawyer and I was forced to let them go. Even if you are an associate of Loukas it is clear that Mr. Christos knew nothing of it. He had only known you for a few hours."

"And what about Cleyton?"

"He has been released also, but he is under orders not to leave Athens. He will be watched." Kravakos leaned forward again. "And now, Mr. Larren, you and I have a lot of talking to do. I want a complete account of your movements since arriving in Athens; where you have been, and who you have talked to. And neither you nor I will get any sleep tonight until we have it all down on paper with your signature at the bottom."

Larren felt his heart sink, for he knew full well that his movements of the last few days were too far outside the law to bear any kind of police investigation. But he managed to get a smile on to his face and pretend his willingness to co-operate.

Kravakos smiled back. "Good, but I have just thought of something that I should have done hours ago." He pushed his chair back and pulled open a drawer in his desk, then, after turning over some forms inside he produced a folded newspaper. "Here," he passed the paper over, "it's an English edition of an Athens paper and it has Loukas's picture on the front page. It's just possible that you have spoken to the man without realizing who he was, and that would clear up everything." He watched Larren's face as he waited for an answer.

Larren stared at the picture of Peter Loukas, but he knew he had never seen the man before. He started to read the caption detailing the Thessaloniki bank raid and had to open the paper farther to read the lower half of the column. Then he saw a name that he did know, and he realized that now it was absolutely vital that he should escape from Kravakos and complete his mission.

The name appeared in a separate news heading and was the name of the man who Smith had claimed was more important than all the scores of paralysed and dying victims held fast by the red death; the man whose knowledge was so valuable that it could sway the balance of world power; the man whom Angelo Valedri had named as part of the blackmail price he wanted in exchange for the Ameytheline antidote.

The news heading stated quite briefly and simply that Professor Eugene Vladomir Andromavitch, the finest scientific brain alive, had vanished.

14

Under Cover of Darkness

Larren read the news paragraph through but it told him nothing more than he had already gleaned from the heading. Andromavitch had simply vanished from his London home and there was no clue to suggest where he might have gone.

However, Larren knew that the scientist's disappearance at this particular moment could not possibly be a coincidence. Angelo Valedri had wanted the man badly for some twisted reason of his own, and regardless of whether Andromavitch had been taken by force, or whether he had been induced to give himself up in order to bring an end to the red death, there was little doubt in Larren's mind that he must now be in Valedri's hands.

Larren had not yet given any thought to the question of why Valedri should need a nuclear scientist, and now he was given no chance to consider the implications of the new move. Kravakos, who had been watching him closely, snapped abruptly, "Well, Larren! Do you know him?"

The demand jolted Larren back to his present position and he remembered that he was supposed to be studying the picture of the wanted Peter Loukas. Regretfully he shook his head, and he hoped that his face revealed no traces of the shock he had just received as he handed the paper back to its owner.

"I'm sorry, Inspector, but I've never seen the man before."

Kravakos sighed. "All right, let us proceed with the statement of your movements."

Larren felt a brief twist of despair wriggle through him, but he realized that the only course he could adopt was to fabricate a false story that would be difficult to either prove or disprove, and set about telling it with as honest an expression as was possible. Where it was possible he told the truth, and the rest he made as short and simple as he was capable; there was less chance of his forgetting it that way, and consequently less chance of Kravakos tripping him up when they went over it again.

For the night of the beach party he substituted an evening stroll through the streets of Athens, and on the previous day, spent on Kyros, he claimed that he had explored the Acropolis. Both lies sounded plausible for a tourist, and with so many fresh holiday-makers swarming over the city and its monuments every day there was no reason why they should be disbelieved. Covering up his two nights in Greece was a much harder task, but he did not think he had been missed from the Hotel Sparta on the first night and blandly stated that he had slept in his own room. The second night, when he had been interrogated by Bruno and Valedri on Kyros, he claimed that he had got drunk and slept it off in his car which he had parked up a side street. That explanation enabled him to include the supposed fall which he insisted had bruised his face, and also provided a reason for him to have returned to his hotel early that morning and slept for the first part of the day.

He knew the story was weak, and as he could obviously find no one to vouch for it, it would hardly stand up as an alibi. But it was the best that he could do and he could only hope that Kravakos would not make too thorough an investigation.

Kravakos slipped in a couple of sharp trick questions during the recital, but Larren knew enough to avoid them and the Inspector eventually listened in silence. When Larren had finished he said, "It is a pity you are staying alone in Athens, for it is clear that there is no one to substantiate all this. However, I will make inquiries at your hotel, and I will try and find this bar where you say you drank too much and fell down. It is another pity that you cannot remember this bar."

Larren said vaguely, "It was near Syntagma Square. That's all I know."

Kravakos scowled. "Even if I find it and there is someone who remembers seeing you, it still will not help me to decide whether or not you were talking to Loukas this afternoon, but you realize that I must start somewhere. Now that an accusation like this has been made I must check your story and your reasons for being here in Athens before I can release you."

Larren looked startled. "But you can't keep me here!"

Kravakos shrugged. "I am sorry, Mr. Larren, but I must detain you overnight at least. You will have to sleep in a cell, but you will be comfortable and I shall provide every courtesy."

Larren knew that the Greek Inspector was playing soft simply because he was completely baffled, and although he seemed prepared to give his prisoner the benefit of the doubt at the moment he was still determined to get to the truth.

Larren began to protest because that was what his part expected of him, but at the same time he knew that he had no choice but to spend the night in the Greek jail.

★ ★ ★

The cell to which Larren was eventually taken was a small, bare-walled room with no windows and a steel door with a narrow, barred inspection panel. The bed was a single palliasse and two grey blankets, and although it was nowhere near as comfortable as Kravakos seemed to think, Larren could have slept there quite satisfactorily in normal circumstances. However, these were no normal circumstances, and Larren felt no desire to sleep. He lay back in the darkness, wondering about Andromavitch and Valedri, and fretting at his own inability to do anything about them.

He fumed in frustrated anger at the hideous mess of complications in which he was now ensnared, and began to seriously wonder whether it was humanly possible to cut through them all and reach Valedri. There was Christos, who was determined to obtain the Ameytheline antidote for his own ends with the help of his self-styled crime syndicate. There was Kravakos desperately trying to establish a connection between Larren and a wanted murderer who was just a name that had been introduced as an excuse to detain him. And finally there was the mysterious Cleyton, who must also fit somewhere into the jigsaw but who so far did not seem to fit into any recognized group. The whole situation seemed to have enveloped Larren like the restraining tentacles of some evil mental octopus, and every disc-like sucker that pulled at his aching brain was tearing at his sanity and leaving behind the indented imprints of a thousand unanswerable question marks.

And meanwhile the red death would still be taking its toll, paralysing and killing in every country in Europe. And the most important nuclear scientist in the western world would be somewhere *en route* to an unknown destination. Events were moving fast and the death roll was getting longer, and Larren was unable to do more than lie in jail and curse the slippery trail that had led him here.

He was still awake at dawn when the grey light began to filter into his cell through the small inspection panel in the door, and he was still no nearer to solving any of his problems. He straightened himself up stiffly, and found that his bruised muscles had congealed again while he relaxed. However, the necessity of getting himself back into shape gave him something to occupy his mind for a few moments and he painfully exercised his limbs until he had loosened up again. His limp had returned when he tried to walk around the cell, and despite an aching stream of protests from his left hip he kept flexing and straightening the leg until he could walk normally once more. Then, deciding that he was as fit as could be expected, he hammered on the door of his cell and demanded breakfast.

A Greek policeman appeared at the small window and curtly told him to wait. Larren tried to tell the man that Kravakos had instructed that he was to be treated courteously, but the policeman spoke hardly any English and simply ignored him. He slammed a small, sliding panel across the inspection slit and walked away. Larren had to wait.

An hour later the cell door opened and the same policeman brought him a meal of bread rolls, jam and coffee. When Larren tried to question him he imparted the information that Inspector Kravakos was out making inquiries, and then left.

Larren ate in gloomy silence and wondered how Kravakos would react when his inquiries produced no tangible results.

He finished his sparse breakfast and then spent an impatient morning in pacing back and forth across his tiny cell. Normally he would have done the sensible thing in this situation, which was to store up some more sleep in readiness for the time when he could move into action again. But for once Larren was unable to relax and sleep.

The time of waiting seemed interminable, but the end, when it came, was swift and unexpected. There was a sudden rattle at the door as a key was twisted in the lock, and then it was pulled open and a burly sergeant stepped back to allow

Kravakos to enter. The Inspector was in full uniform again and he was smiling somewhat uncomfortably.

"Good morning, Mr. Larren. I trust that you slept well."

Larren nodded without answering.

Kravakos looked ill at ease but he continued to smile. "I have an apology to make, Mr. Larren. This morning I received a report from a small village near the Albanian frontier which definitely indicates that the wanted man, Peter Loukas, is hiding in the mountains in that area. Therefore it is impossible for him to have been here in Athens yesterday afternoon, and you could not possibly have been seen talking to him. So I must concede that you are telling the truth and that the man who called himself Cleyton was lying. Especially as I have just learned that Cleyton is no longer available to answer any questions. He appears to have fled in order to avoid being arrested for obstructing the police."

Larren was too taken back to answer and Kravakos went on. "There is still something about this affair that I do not like Mr. Larren, for I still want to know why Cleyton lied to me. If I find him I intend to discover exactly what his motives were. Meanwhile I have no cause to continue to hold you, and although I must ask you not to leave Athens until the matter has been properly explained, you are now free to go."

Larren didn't argue. He could hardly believe that he was getting out of jail that easily.

★ ★ ★

It was noon when Larren walked out of the police station, and the sky above Athens was hot, blue and cloudless. Larren was still thanking the fortunate twist of relenting fate that had brought about his freedom once more, and he was almost tempted to make for the nearest bar for a much needed celebration drink. Then he remembered his mission and hailed a taxi to take him down to Tourkolimano harbour instead.

He stopped the taxi and paid off the driver just before the small boat harbour

256

came into sight and then walked back to the side street where he had left his own Renault. He approached the car cautiously, for fate had sprung so many surprises upon him since his arrival in Greece that he was becoming doubly wary in everything he did. However the car was still there, there was no one waiting for him inside and it was not even booby-trapped. He began to hope that his luck was changing at last.

He unlocked the car door and slid behind the wheel, and then, before doing anything else, he thrust his hand under the driving seat and groped around until his fingers encountered his automatic and the other items he had hidden there. He removed them one by one and transferred them back to his person. He was realizing now that if Kravakos had found him in possession of those arms he would still be under arrest, but even so he promised himself that he was not separating from his knife and his automatic again. He recalled making that promise to himself before, but this time he meant to keep it — even if somebody had to die for it.

Grimly he started the engine of the Renault and drove away.

He knew exactly what he had to do, for regardless of all the complications the main issue was still clear. His job was to kill Valedri and get the Ameytheline antidote back to Smith, and he didn't need the answers to any questions to do that. He could concentrate on solving the surrounding puzzles afterwards.

He still needed a boat of some kind to take him out to Kyros, but he knew better now than to continue his search around Tourkolimano. Instead he decided that he would have to try some smaller harbour along the coast, and consequently drove fast along the familiar coast road towards Sounion Head. As the car left Athens and passed the entrance to the airport he was trying to convince himself that Christos could not possibly have friends in all the harbours along the coast.

He passed the villa, where he had rescued Carla Valedri from her kidnappers, but he barely spared a glance for the sun-bleached building in its pine-shaded grounds. He knew that it would hold nothing of interest now. The road continued to follow the sea and swept past a never-ending panorama of sandy beaches and rocky coves, sometimes separated by dunes or pines, and sometimes close enough for Larren to pick out the individual pebbles on the sea bed below the crystal-clear waters. However, Larren's only thoughts lay in scanning the small harbours that he passed for a likely-looking launch.

None of the harbours seemed to offer anything that might be of use, and he was beginning to think that his change of luck had already deserted him when the road suddenly swung round an idyllic little bay. Above the beach was a large new bungalow motel, and stretching out into the tranquil waters of the bay itself was a small, white-painted jetty with several sailing craft and two or three launches moored alongside. Larren realized that the boats must belong to the motel, and were in all probability available to its customers, and without hesitation he swung the Renault on to the motel car park.

It seemed that the motel was also a restaurant and a night club and the reception desk was inside the bar. Larren made inquiries, and after awaiting the arrival of a short, waddling little man who was the manager and spoke hesitant English, he found that his first guess had been right. The boats, beach and jetty were all privately owned by the motel, and were available only to residents. Larren promptly booked a room for three nights, just to show good faith, and then arranged to hire one of the launches for an evening cruise along the coast. After some argument he persuaded the man that he did not need a guide and would much prefer to go alone.

Three hours later Larren stood at the wheel of a fifteen-foot motor launch and headed it out into the Aegean along a pathway of burning gold spangles that danced in a stream of lowering rays from the setting sun. The golden sea was a blinding mirror and his eyes were screwed into narrow slits below the low peak of a borrowed cap he had found in the launch's tiny cabin. The deck-boards surged powerfully beneath his feet and he felt that nothing could possibly stop him now. Soon that sun would be sinking into the sea and he would be landing on Kyros under the embracing cover of darkness, and now that he was actually on the first lap of his long-planned murder raid he felt supremely confident. All the beatings and interrogations he had endured during the past two or three days had stemmed from attempting to play a part that did not fit him; the part of the uncomprehending tourist. He had been forced to take a savage amount of punishment to maintain that part, but now he was through with acting. He was returning instead to his natural role. The role of the trained and expert killer. His grey-green eyes began to glitter slightly at the thought.

He knew the general location of Kyros, and with the position of the dying sun to guide him he did not expect any trouble in finding it. In any case the launch was well topped-up with fuel so he had plenty to spare if he should have to spend some time in searching. His present starting point was much nearer to the island than Tourkolimano had been, and he anticipated a trip of something just under two hours. By that time the sun should be below the horizon.

In actual fact it proved to be just over the two hours before he finally sighted Kyros. The sun had touched the sea and set it afire with orange flame before fading slowly from sight, and now the Aegean was a dark and forbidding charcoal-grey beneath a twilight sky. Kyros rose from its brooding surface like a single, stumpy molar tooth, no longer bright and green but black and menacing in the night.

Larren regarded the island grimly and cut the throttles of the launch until the engine died from a lusty roar into a gentle throb. He drifted nearer to the rising tooth of land and turned the launch in a wide circle that brought him round to the steep cliffs on the north side of the island. He could see the high pinnacle of rock that Carla had pointed out as the sanctuary to the sea god Poseidon etched clearly against the sky and he steered slowly towards it. Here Carla had said that the steep rock walls were unclimbable and so Larren was hoping that Valedri did not consider it necessary to watch the sea approaches on this side as he allowed the launch to creep in with her engine barely turning.

The night was complete now but for a faint glimmer of starlight and Larren smiled softly to himself as he cut the engines altogether to let the launch drift the last few yards beneath the looming cliffs. The sea was breaking on the rocks below the sheer walls, but it was a calm sea with no real waves, and despite the sound of slapping water and the soft gurgles of foam there was no danger of the launch being smashed or capsized. Larren's keen gaze searched the line of breaking water until he found a jagged snout of rock to which he could secure the mooring rope, and then he removed his jacket and slipped over the side into the dark sea.

The water was pleasantly warm and he pulled himself across the intervening gap in two quick strokes and deftly lashed the rope around the rock. The launch was now moored close below the cliffs and he doubted whether anyone looking down from the cliff top would be able to detect it in the shadows.

He pulled himself back aboard the launch and stared up at the perpendicular walls. They were smooth-worn and slippery, and as Carla had said they would be impossible to climb. But Larren remained unperturbed, for at this point he had no intention of attempting to climb.

He stood upright and quickly stripped off his clothes, tying them into a small tight bundle with his automatic wrapped up in the middle. Then he tied the bundle loosely around his neck so that it rested lightly on his back just above his shoulder blades. Finally he lowered himself back over the side and turned away from the launch, swimming with slow, strength-conserving strokes along the foot of the cliffs.

He knew he had quite a way to swim before the cliffs ended and he reached the single beach where he could climb up, but he was an excellent swimmer and he knew that he could cover the distance without any undue exertion. On a previous mission he had once swam twelve miles from the Chinese coast to a waiting submarine with a radio on his back, and compared to that this would be a pleasure paddle.

The salt water proved to be a pleasant balm to the display of bruises that he had collected during his short stay in Greece and he found that he was enjoying his nocturnal swim. The high cliffs drowned him in shadow and he moved like some deadly, lazing shark through the calm waters. His bundle of clothing had settled comfortably on his back, and although it was gradually getting wetter he did not mind. He had stripped mostly because it left him more freedom to swim and as long as the sea did not penetrate and soak his automatic he was not bothered.

An hour passed, an hour during which he never once changed his smooth, steady stroke, and then at last he came in sight of the beach. The cliffs had descended from a sheer one-hundred-foot barrier to a stiff climb of less than fifty feet, and

Larren decided that it was now time he landed, for if possible he did not want to swim right up to the beach.

He pulled himself out of the water on to a sloping rock face that angled up to the cliff wall and relaxed there a moment in order to pick his path. The night air was cold now upon his naked skin, but he dismissed the discomfort with barely a thought. He decided that there was a fair chance that he could make it to the cliff top from his present position if he could once get up above the lower rocks that were slippery with spray, and slowly he began to inch his way upwards.

The harsh rock scratched at his naked body, but in bare feet he found that he could still grip reasonably well and he made slow but definite progress. Once he slipped back, but his fingertips held in a narrow fissure and enabled him to check his fall. Panting slightly he began to drag himself back to his original position, and after a few more sticky minutes he found that the rock was dry beneath him and that he was above the slippery stretch. He gave himself a moment to re-capture his breath and then started again. The climb became suddenly simple and a few moments later he was wriggling over the cliff edge and lying on the wet grass.

There was no sign of life, but Larren knew that Valedri had trained guard dogs patrolling the isand and he was taking no chances. He squirmed on his belly into a nearby hollow and swiftly scrambled back into his clothes, they clung wetly to his damp body, but his precious automatic was still bone dry. Larren felt more competent now that he was dressed and carefully bound up his left hand and arm in his jacket. Then he took his automatic in his left hand and his sheath knife in his right and decided that he was now capable of dealing with any guard dog. He left the hollow and began to move inland.

He covered half the distance towards Valedri's villa before one of the guard dogs found him. He heard a single, snarling bark from his right that was immediately followed by the sound of the brute hurling itself towards him. Larren spun round to see the dark shape coming at him with the speed of a leaping panther. He could never have hit that flying target on the move, and although he flung up his left arm and pointed the automatic he had no intention of firing. The dog was a massive wolfhound, and for one horrible moment Larren thought that it had been trained solely to kill and was coming for his throat. He saw a flash of white teeth and splashes of the dog's slaver hit him in the face as the brute attacked. He went down with the snarling wolfhound on top of him, but the brute had done exactly what it had been trained to do and had seized his cloth-bound gun hand.

Larren rolled desperately with his left wrist clamped hard in the dog's wrenching jaws, and with one frantic effort he thrust his arm away, pushing the dog's head up and revealing the sleek line of its throat as it reared above him. The razor-edged sheath knife in his right hand moved in a gleaming arc and then plunged deep into its intended target.

The stricken wolfhound writhed madly,

but with Larren's wrist still blocking its jaws and the knife twisting in its throat the animal could only gurgle helplessly as it died. It collapsed on top of Larren and he squirmed his face away frenziedly as he tasted the hot spurt of blood that erupted from the torn throat.

Breathing harshly Larren disentangled himself from the dead guard dog and retrieved his knife. In the same moment he shook his left wrist free of the protecting jacket and picked up the automatic he had been forced to drop when the wolfhound had attacked.

Seconds later he was crouching silently in the shadow of a low bush a few yards away and waiting with his knife once more at the ready.

He was waiting for the dog's handler, for if the man came searching for his missing companion and found the corpse he would most certainly give the alarm. That was something which Larren could not afford, and if he was to succeed with his night's work then the handler must die also.

He had already literally tasted blood,

269

and his grey-green killer's eyes were gleaming brightly as he waited for the man to appear. So far he had lost every round that had been played, but now he was paying back the score.

15

The Wraith that Killed

Nothing stirred under Larren's probing gaze as he carefully examined his surroundings in the night. Behind him the Aegean lay like a vast enveloping sea of ink below the cliff tops; to his left the ground ran down in a grassy slope to the narrow beach and the small landing stage, and to his right the cliffs rose gradually higher towards the lofty, unseen pillar of rock that marked the sanctuary of Poseidon. Somewhere ahead and again to his left lay Valedri's villa in its sheltering dip in the hills, but as yet he could not distinguish it in the darkness. The night sky above him was moonless and thin clouds were filtering across to cut the dim glimmer of starlight.

Larren could still feel the wolfhound's blood lying moist and warm on his cheek but he did not move to wipe it away. He was sure that the dog must have had a handler and that man could appear at any moment, and he dared not move on and leave him alive.

He began to shiver slightly in his wet clothes, and the soft breeze was suddenly cold on the exposed parts of his skin. His left leg was beginning to get cramped and he had to resist the strong temptation to change his position. The blood on his face was congealing and irritating his cheek and he had to crush down another rising urge to wipe it away.

The minutes of waiting followed each other with dragging reluctance until at last Larren began to think that he must have made a mistake and that the wolfhound had been let loose to roam the cliff tops alone, but still he took no chances and remained motionless. He could ill afford to lose these precious minutes of darkness but he had to be absolutely sure that the guard dog had not been prowling on the loose before he continued with his long-planned mission of murder.

The cramp in his leg became a twisting torment that spread down his badly bruised hip, and he was almost on the point of giving in to the need to ease it when his eyes registered a vague impression of movement in the night. Then from the same direction came a soft, insistent whisper that carried clearly in the stillness.

Larren endured the nagging cramping pains in his leg and crouched lower into the meagre pool of shadow beside the half-concealing bush. The persistent voice called again through the darkness and Larren knew that the still invisible dog handler was approaching warily as he tried to locate his dead pet.

The man was somewhere on Larren's left, coming up from the beach, and he heard the dog's name hissed once more as the man came nearer. There was a note of alarm in the urgent whisper now, and Larren knew that the man was suspicious as well as wary. Then he saw the dim outline of the advancing guard as he came up the gentle slope.

Gently Larren laid his automatic in the grass and his muscles tensed as he moved his knife hand under the cover of his open shirt. There would be no revealing glitter of steel to warn the man that he was walking into a trap. He was only ten yards away now and Larren saw his mouth open to repeat his worried call, then he saw the black, huddled shape of the dead wolfhound. A startled ejaculation of alarm slipped through the half open lips, and the guard moved swiftly towards the still corpse. He held a large and very lethal-looking automatic in his right hand.

He passed within four feet of the low bush that offered Larren's only place of concealment, and he leaned forward slightly in order to recognize his pet. He swore sharply and started to turn, but Larren had already moved silently to his feet behind him. The guard sensed his danger even though Larren had closed in without as much as disturbing the air, and his uncertain movement became a sudden desperate twist as he tried to bring his body round in a fast whirl. But by then he was already drawing his last terrified breath, for Larren's right hand locked round his mouth to shut off any outcry and at the same time pulled back hard. As the guard's head went back so his throat was exposed, and he died in exactly the same way as his four-footed partner, the knife blade thrusting into his vulnerable neck and cutting outwards to sever the windpipe in one proficient stroke.

Slowly Larren lowered the body to the ground beside the dead wolfhound and then turned it face upwards with his foot. He recognized the features as those of one of the hard-faced men he had seen lounging on the beach during his previous visit to Kyros. The man's open throat made a gruesome picture even in the dim blackness, but Larren had often seen worse. This was the second man he had killed since his arrival in Greece, but this time there was no regret. When he thought of the creeping, paralysing horror of the red death that this man and his fellows were helping Valedri to spread his heart was empty of any trace of pity.

Turning away he retrieved his own automatic and his jacket from the grass, and again he wrapped the jacket carefully around his left arm in case he should encounter another of the guard dogs. He didn't think that there would be two man and dog teams patrolling the same stretch of cliff but he was taking no chances. Again he held the automatic in his left hand as he moved off, while the knife, the only weapon he intended to use unless the alarm was raised, was gripped ready for instant use in his right. He didn't even look back at the bodies he left behind him but moved down towards the low beach like a wraith in the night, a silent and exceedingly deadly wraith who would not hesitate to kill when necessary.

He knew that approaching the beach would be dangerous, for down there there would probably be another guard. But only by making his assault from that direction could he be sure of finding the high voltage trip wire that he had spotted on his first visit. He knew that the wire would undoubtedly surround the whole of the villa, and if he failed to avoid it the merest touch would fry him to death.

He reached the soft sand of the beach,

and wiping his knife clean on his shirt sleeve he gripped the blade in his teeth as he snaked along on his elbows and belly. He could neither see nor hear any indication of another guard, but on the open beach it would be foolish to take the risk of standing up.

The moment of cramp had passed now that he was moving once more and for that he was thankful. His confidence had been boosted high by his successful encounter with the first line of Valedri's defences, and he had to remind himself firmly that haste and a single wrong move could still bring his progress to an abrupt and final halt. Now that he was this close to Valedri it would be madness to fail through any lack of the proper precautions.

He made himself move more slowly as he crossed the beach, and when he was level with the jetty he turned inland and began to squirm his way towards the villa. His eyes were fully accustomed to the night now and he found that he could just determine the outline of the building with its square, modern angles. As he closed in

277

the sand beneath him gave way to low, gently rippling dunes that were scattered with tufts of coarse dry grass. Soon the sand gave way altogether and the ground became all grass. Larren's pace became slower still for he knew that he must be almost on top of the electrified wire.

When he had first spotted the wire he had marked its position in his memory with the help of a small hillock just behind it, and now he strained his eyes over the terrain ahead in an effort to locate the hillock again. He was certain that he was following the same track along which Bruno had led Carla and himself up to the villa, but to his dismay he could see no sign of the vital landmark that he needed to locate the wire.

Slowly and tentatively he continued to inch his way forwards. The sand had clung in muddy patches to his wet clothing and many of the fine grains had penetrated to irritate his skin. His heart-beat was verging upon panic at the thought of what that sliver of wire could do if he were to stumble upon it accidentally, and his palms were beginning to sweat. His teeth ached where they clamped upon the blade of his knife and his eyes ached with the strain as he searched the ground in front of him.

Then he saw it, a small grassy knoll like a miniature ant hill, a few yards ahead and well over to his left.

He drank down relief like a rejuvenating wine as he realized that he was to the right of the track and manœuvred himself back on course with deft movements of his elbows, hips and toes. The tiny hillock, not much more than a bump on the ground, had been approximately four feet behind the wire, and when Larren was within six feet of it he stopped.

He stared into the grass immediately before him, and even though he knew that the wire had to be under his nose he couldn't see it. He closed his eyes for a few seconds to ease them and then looked again, but still he could see nothing but the long dry grass.

Very carefully he moved his left hand to smooth the thick grass blades to one side, his fingertips were tingling with anticipation and his hands were oozing sweat. He moved his fingers forward another two inches and felt his heart jumping violently. Then he saw it, a slender thread of silver less than six inches from his hand and barely visible in the darkness.

Cautiously he rose to his hands and knees and passed the upper half of his body over the wire, for a second he bridged it with the high voltage current flowing only inches below his belly, and then he brought each knee over in turn.

He moved on and this time the flow of relief left him feeling weak and almost dizzy. He had to stop and shut his eyes for a moment before he could strengthen his sagging muscles and continue his stealthy, snakelike approach to the villa. He covered the last sixty yards with every expectation of finding another guard, but the night was disturbingly empty. Now that he was close to the villa he passed beneath the decorative pine and olive trees that were planted thinly around, and he lay in the stygian blackness beneath one of the olives until he had convinced himself that he was still alone in the night.

His next difficulty now lay in entering the villa and locating Valedri, for he had no idea which room was the old man's bedroom. The problem revolved in his mind but he knew that there were only two ways of finding his quarry; one was to search blindly and try every bedroom in the villa until he hit the right one, and the other was to make someone tell him what he wanted to know. The first he dismissed as being too risky, for even with his skill he knew that he could never search the whole villa without raising the alarm. In a normal household it might have been possible, but not among a small army of well-recruited bodyguards. The second method seemed by far his best angle of attack, and as he had no intention of deliberately tangling with any of the guards that could be avoided he was left with a choice of Carla or Antonella. Carla, as far as he knew, was still infatuated with him and might be useful later, but from what little he had seen of Antonella he had formed the impression that she was not as loyal to her ageing lover as she should be. Without hesitation he chose Antonella.

She had told him that her room was at the far end of the corridor that ran outside his own bedroom, and he also remembered that the corridor had ended in a large window that opened on to a balcony, and with this in mind he began to worm his way silently around to the side of the building. Here his probing gaze located the outline of the balcony half-way along the wall and some ten feet above ground level.

Larren wriggled closer and saw that the wall was smooth and that there were no cracks or footholds that would enable him to climb up. He cursed softly and then began to circle away until he could straighten up beside the bole of a tall, spreading pine some ten yards from the wall. Again he made absolutely sure that he was still alone before he moved. When he was satisfied he re-donned the crumpled jacket that was still wrapped around his left arm and slipped his automatic into the pocket.

His knife went back into its sheath and then he sprinted swiftly towards the balcony and jumped. His hands clamped on the bottom of the railings and he pulled himself up and over in one fast, scrambling heave. He dropped flat on to his face, withdrawing his knife instantly and freezing into stillness.

There was no sound. No alarm. Nobody had witnessed his flying leap.

Carefully Larren rose to his feet and inspected the tall french windows behind him, and here fate was again relenting in apology for the vicious way she had treated him at first, for the windows were already slightly open. Larren guessed that Valedri was so sure of his outer defences that he had felt quite safe in leaving the windows ajar to allow the fresh air to circulate, for this far south a sealed house would have been unbearably stuffy. Larren blessed his good fortune and gently eased the windows open a fraction wider until he could slip inside.

From his trouser pocket he produced another item of his standard equipment, a small pencil torch which he flashed guardedly around the corridor. Antonella had said that her room was at this end, but as there were rooms leading off both sides of the corridor he still had a choice of two. So far he had been bearing left all night as he circled the island, and so far he had been lucky, and although he was not consciously thinking this he almost instinctively turned left again.

He switched off his torch once he had located the door, and then he turned the handle very softly. He eased the door open an inch and listened. After a few seconds his ears picked up the barely audible sound of regular breathing. Slowly he pushed the door until he could squeeze into the bedroom. The soft, even pace of the sleeper's breathing did not alter and he knew that his presence was not even suspect. He closed the door behind him and again pressed the switch on his torch. The tiny beam angled down towards the carpet and it had been specially made so that it switched on and off with no betraying click.

Larren moved the torch cautiously about the room and then settled the beam on a small footstool beside the bed. A black brassière and a very brief pair of black panties, both trimmed with wisps of red lace lay on the stool, and he knew without beaming his torch into the sleeper's eyes that he had found Antonella.

Carefully he approached the bed and shone the torch on the lower end. The small circle of light picked out a shapely pair of feet close together, and he realized that as it was a warm night Antonella was lying on top of the sheets. He moved the torch higher, tracing the outline of trim ankles and neat calves. She was lying partly on her side and her body was bent into an S shape at the hips and knees. He caught his breath for a moment as the torch beam moved along the smooth golden line of her thighs, and then he saw that she was wearing a short, baby doll negligee that reached her hips but might as well not have bothered. The beam played higher to pick out the swelling curves of her breasts below the transparent material, and then he laid it gently on the bed beside her. He had seen enough to tell him where her head was positioned and the first she knew of his presence was the steel hand clamping down over her mouth and the sharp, biting caress of the knife-point pricking her throat.

Her body writhed instinctively on the bed, shocked into sudden terrified wakefulness. Larren held her down firmly and commanded softly, "Keep still, Antonella. I want some information and provided that I get it I won't harm you, but if you decide to scream I'll simply push this knife home and try elsewhere."

Antonella stopped her feverish twisting and her body became stiff with fear. Larren sensed the panicky heaving of her breasts even though he could not see them, and he could hear her breath rasping harshly in her throat.

He went on quietly. "I think you're a sensible girl, Antonella, so I'm going to take my hand from your mouth so we can talk. Please don't disappoint me by doing anything foolish."

He removed his hand and felt for

the torch that he had laid beside her. Finding it he switched it on and saw her face, white with fear, staring up at him from the pillow. Her bronze-red waves reflected the rays of the tiny beam, and although her eyes were wide open he still could not define their colour.

He said, "In case you haven't guessed, this is Simon Larren. And all I want to know is the position of the room where Valedri sleeps."

At the mention of Valedri's name some of the colour returned to Antonella's cheeks and part of her fear was dispelled. And Larren knew that she was realizing that despite her own highly delicate position, his was almost as dangerous. Her red lips formed a very hesitant smile as she replied softly.

"Valedri will kill you for this, Larren. You should never have come back."

Larren said calmly, "Let me worry about that. All I want from you are directions on where to find Valedri. Afterwards I shall have to ensure that you remain here safe and secure, but I won't harm you and someone will undoubtedly release you in the morning."

Antonella was becoming braver and her face was almost back to normal. "Why didn't you ask little Carla?" she asked. "Surely she would be the one to help you. Just pop into her bed for five minutes and she'd probably do anything for you."

Larren said flatly, "I think Carla is loyal to her father — but I have my doubts about you." He moved the knife-point just enough to scare her and demanded, "Now tell me where Valedri's room is. I don't have a lot of time to waste."

Antonella flinched and then became still again. "I was right about you, wasn't I, Larren? I knew you were no ordinary amateur." Those undefinable eyes gazed up at him calmly and she went on. "But I don't think you're good enough to get away with this. Angelo's bedroom is on the right at the other end of the corridor, the second one from the end. I'll tell you because it won't make damn all difference in the long run, and I don't see why I should stick my neck out in the meantime."

Larren said grimly, "If I don't find

Valedri in that room I'll come straight back. I hope you realize that."

"You'll find him, and I hope for your sake that he kills you quickly."

Larren removed the knife from her throat without answering, and she watched him uncertainly as he pulled a long length of cord from his pocket. He ordered her to roll over and she obeyed without a murmur as he secured her wrists behind her. He was working swiftly now, and pulling one of the sheets from beneath her he knotted it about her ankles. Finally he took the loose end of cord that trailed from her wrists and pulling her head back he tied it in a slack noose about her neck. She began to wriggle in protest but he silenced her with a soft warning.

"If you attempt to move about after I've gone you'll strangle yourself," he whispered grimly. "So just lay still and you'll be all right."

Antonella said bitterly, "You're a real expert aren't you?"

Larren again didn't bother to answer. Instead he tore two strips off another of the sheets and deftly gagged her so that she could make no sound. Then he beamed his torch over her figure to survey his handiwork. He smiled and murmured softly.

"Goodnight, Antonella, and pleasant dreams."

Her eyes radiated a strange, controlled hatred that should have been completely alien in such an enticing body, and she made no attempt to move as he turned away. His torch beam accidently shone up her bared thighs as he passed and he had to force the torch away and concentrate on his next move. He did not know whether Antonella had been telling the truth or whether she had only given him directions that would lead him into some kind of trap. But there was only one way to find out.

He closed the door of Antonella's bedroom behind him and moved on down the corridor, the pencil torch again exploring ahead of him. When he reached the second door from the end on the right he stood beside it for long moments with his ears straining to catch any sound. Then at last he extinguished the torch again and tried the door. It opened with silent ease.

He inched his way inside and immediately heard the harsh breathing of a heavy sleeper. Caution forced him to wait a few minutes more, and then he exchanged his knife for his automatic and moved closer to the bed. He shone his torch directly on to the sleeping man's face and felt a surge of elation as he recognized the swarthy features of the man he had come to kill. And before Valedri could blink into wakefulness he brought the butt of his automatic down on the man's temple in a savage knock-out blow.

16

The Man with the
Ballet Dancer Figure

It was night, and Piraeus, the thriving
port of Athens and the main shipping
centre of Greece was quiet and almost
deserted. There were a few pools of
light and sluggish activity around some
of the larger sea-going freighters that
were preparing for departure, but most
of the vessels were still and silent and
carrying the minimum of lights. The
large, sleek-lined ferries that trafficked
between Piraeus, Patras and Brindisi, and
their smaller sisters who carried tourists
to and fro between the Aegean islands
were all motionless at their berths. In
one of the more remote corners of the
docks a small fleet of six forty-foot fishing
boats were moored. They were all built
to the same design; two short masts
and a cramped, paint-flaking wheelhouse

that was not much larger than a sentry box, their decks were littered with rolled bundles of netting and smelled of the flaking scales of long dead fish. A man was climbing down from the quay to board one of the fishing boats, a craft with the name *Xenia* painted on its bows, he was a Greek, young and darkly handsome and holding his left arm stiffly as though it had been recently injured. Thirty yards away, hidden completely by the black shadow of a warehouse wall, stood a second man, silently watching; he was a tall, slim man, also young and with the supple, graceful figure of a male ballet dancer. The young Greek was Savino, and the man with the ballet dancer figure was the mysterious Adrian Cleyton.

Cleyton had been watching Savino from the moment he had witnessed the young Greek arriving with a lawyer to extract Christos and Dimitri from the police station. The man in whom he was really interested was Christos, but keeping watch on that deadly blue-jawed professional would be far too dangerous now that he had been forced to reveal his identity by rescuing Larren from the launch, and he felt that it was much safer to keep Savino under surveillance in his place. He knew now that Christos and Savino were brothers and that they were in this venture together, and he reasoned that if he was on the right track then one could lead him to the end of the trail just as easily as the other.

Cleyton knew that he had taken a grave risk in showing his face to Christos and Dimitri, and an equally grave one in stirring up Kravakos and the Greek police, but despite the risks he had had very good reasons for wanting Simon Larren to remain alive. When he had trailed Larren to Tourkolimano he had been an unseen spectator to the approach of the boy Nico, and he had watched as the British agent was led aboard the launch. When Nico returned ashore alone he had been counting the roll of grubby notes that Christos had thrown at his feet, and Cleyton knew instinctively that Larren had walked into a trap.

Nico had walked away from the

harbour, cutting across the wide main road that ran south to parallel the Atki Apollon coastline and heading up a narrow side street. A few minutes later he turned into an even narrower street where the unpaved surface was of dusty, hard-packed earth. On either side ran a row of unattractive houses with the faded yellow whitewash flaking from their plastered walls.

The time was mid-afternoon and there was no one about, for at this hour the inhabitants preferred to doze in the shade to escape the uncomfortable heat. Nico was no exception, and his only thoughts were of sleeping away the sluggish hours until the tavernas became lively again in the evening. He climbed the three concrete steps to the doorway of the building where he occupied a single, disgustingly filthy room and let himself into the small hallway. The hallway was dark and dingy and quite empty, and the house was silent and breathed no sign of life.

Nico had been taken completely by surprise by what happened next, and all that he ever saw of his attacker was the slim, delicately manicured hand that abruptly appeared under his nose and closed over his mouth. The hand looked almost smooth and elegant enough to belong to a woman, but there was a supple strength there that made it impossible for him to cry out, and that and the powerful grip that had forced his right arm up between his shoulder blades had held him as helpless as a child.

Nico had been thrust deeper into the dingy hallway and heard the door kicked into place behind him. His arm was twisted ruthlessly to near breaking point, and the fierce pain combined with the even finer agony of blind unreasoning fear made him willing to talk even before the soft, demanding voice began to murmur by his ear.

Cleyton had assessed the youth's moral character well, and in less than two minutes he knew that what he had feared was fact; Simon Larren had been marked down for death. Seconds later Nico had been skilfully silenced with a sharp palm blow and was left unconscious in a corner of the hallway as Cleyton hurried back to Tourkolimano.

To his dismay he found that Christos's launch had already sailed and for a moment he was in a quandary. Then had spotted a patrolling policeman idly pacing his beat, and he had realized that his only hope of saving Larren's life now was to enlist the resources of the Athens police. However, he could hardly tell them the truth and for a moment he was at a loss to create a story strong enough to send them in pursuit of the launch. Then he remembered the picture that had been in all the Greek papers that morning, and on impulse he decided to use the name of the wanted Thessaloniki bank bandit.

Later he had deliberately left his hotel and made himself scarce, knowing that in the face of his disappearance and the complete lack of any real evidence Kravakos would eventually be forced to release Larren from jail.

Now Cleyton relaxed in the darkness at Piraeus and felt calmly pleased with himself as he waited for Savino to return from his nocturnal visit aboard the *Xenia*.

He had a long while to wait, but Cleyton was a patient man. Savino had vanished into the small wheel-house and had presumably descended to the tiny cabin below, and when he finally re-appeared again there was a second man with him. They stood on deck for a moment and shook hands, and then Savino climbed back on to the quay and began to stride briskly away along the dock-side. Cleyton watched him go and then turned his attention to the second man who still remained aboard the fishing boat.

He was a short but lusty-looking man who would probably be somewhere in his forties, dressed in rough, work-stained trousers and an old blue jersey. Like most Greeks he favoured a small moustache, and he was bare-headed. He watched Savino leave, then he abruptly glanced down at something in his hand, smiled, and then pulled himself nimbly on to the quay and moved off in the opposite direction.

Cleyton reasoned that the man must be the captain of the *Xenia*, and he had a deep suspicion that the something in his hand had been a roll of notes. He hesitated a moment, and then decided that he could always pick up Savino's trail later. Right now he wanted to find out what the young Greek had wanted from the captain of the fishing boat.

Without any further delay he began to follow the second man through the docks.

The *Xenia*'s captain led him away from the quayside and eventually turned into a small, somewhat unsavoury little taverna. Here, just inside the open door, was a large glass showcase containing eggs, tomatoes, oddments of thick sliced sausage, plates of half-cooked fish and several large crabs and lobsters. Behind the showcase pans of fried potatoes and reeking cabbage simmered on a cramped cooking range, and the whole place smelled of cooking oil. The stocky fisherman studied the showcase for a moment and then pointed out the plate of fish he fancied and gestured towards the pans. Then, while his meal was being prepared, he ordered a glass of wine from the bar at the back end of the taverna and sat down to wait.

Cleyton watched him through the open door from a discreet distance, frowning thoughtfully and then abruptly making up his mind. He strolled casually into the taverna with a half-simple grin on his face, nodded amiably at the sour-faced man who was preparing the food, and at the same time neatly allowed his right hip to collide solidly with the table where the fishing captain sat. The single glass of pale yellow retzina wine rocked jerkily and tipped over to roll tinkling to the floor. The stocky man lurched to his feet and swore angrily.

Cleyton's grin vanished and he stammered with embarrassment as he sought to placate the man by buying more wine. At one early stage of his career he had trained as an actor and this was not the first time that that training had come in useful in his present trade. By holding his breath as his hands moved ineffectually to dab up the spilled wine, he even managed to colour his face a convincing red as the blood flushed his

300

cheeks, and by the time the wine-glass had been re-filled he had the simple fisherman feeling almost sorry for him.

When everything had settled he sat down at the table and began to apologize yet again, for another of his talents lay in the fact that he had a flair for languages, and among six others, one of which included perfect Russian, he spoke fluent modern Greek. The fishing captain had now given way to amusement at his worried insistence and waved the words aside.

Cleyton allowed himself to relax and adopted the manner of one who having invited a conversation was not quite sure how to go about it. He introduced himself under the name of Hector and described himself as steward from one of the larger ferries that cruised between Greece and Italy, a description that fitted his smooth hands and tidy appearance as well as explaining his presence in this less refined area of the docks. The *Xenia*'s captain gave his name as Panapopolis.

The meal arrived that Panapopolis had ordered and he hungrily began to eat, his new companion insisted on refilling his wine glass again and under the mellowing influence of the bitter retzina he began to feel content. He warmed slowly towards this uncertain but friendly Hector who, now that they were talking on friendly terms, was wistfully revealing a secret desire to go to sea as something more worthwhile than a waiter on a floating restaurant. Panapopolis began to tell deliberately tall tales about fishing and the sea, talking with his mouth full and colouring his words with grand gestures of his hands. He was in a good humour now and quite suddenly he decided that this eager young steward was actually envious, a fact that tickled his vanity and made him more amiable still.

The wine continued to flow in pace with Panapopolis's contented conversation, and when the eager Hector tentatively asked if he could accompany him on a fishing trip one night the *Xenia*'s captain was almost inclined to agree. Then he shrugged his shoulders and said apologetically, "If I were fishing tonight I would take you out, my friend. But tonight I have already hired out my boat to a man named Savino who wants me to take himself and some friends out to sea, so I cannot take you along."

Hector's face saddened. "But you will still need a crew," he said hopefully.

Panapopolis shook his head. "No, this is not to be a fishing trip. What its purpose is I do not know, but Mr. Savino insists that I must bring no crew but myself, and that if I need any help one of his men will assist me." He grinned widely. "This I do not mind, for Mr. Savino pays well and I shall not have to share out the money."

Hector's eyes widened with excitement. "It sounds very mysterious," he whispered.

Panapopolis was amused by the conspiratorial tone, and his natural vanity coupled with the wine he had drunk induced him to enlarge upon the subject. "As you say, my friend, it is mysterious. This Mr. Savino and his friends will board my boat in less than an hour, and then I must take them out to sea where we will rendezvous with a motor launch which I must follow — and

I do not know where it is going."

"Is this not dangerous?" asked Hector in a worried tone. "Or perhaps you know this Savino well?"

"No, I have never met him before tonight. But the pay is high so the risk I am prepared to take. There is no reason why any harm should befall me."

From there the conversation flowed into less exciting channels, and they sipped another slow glass of retzina wine before Panapopolis realized that it was time he hurried back to his boat to make the last-minute preparations for putting to sea. He shook hands with the friendly Hector and they wished each other luck before he left. As he walked away from the taverna Panapopolis was thinking that the ship's steward was quite a pleasant young fellow, despite his clumsiness and his unquestioning gullibility.

Five minutes later as he passed through a particularly black and lonely section of the docks Panapopolis heard a slight sound behind him. He hesitated a second, and then decided that it must be a rat and carried on. Almost simultaneously something exploded just behind his left ear and he toppled unconscious to the ground.

The man with the ballet dancer figure looked down at him and felt a strong sense of distaste at his own actions as he massaged the cutting edge of his right palm, and then he swiftly set to work to secure the fishing captain's wrists and ankles with a set of cords from his pocket. Afterwards he added an effective gag and almost tenderly dragged the unfortunate Panapopolis into a concealed corner formed by some packing cases standing against a warehouse wall.

The façade of the insipid Hector had vanished now, and it was Adrian Cleyton who walked out of the shadows and headed swiftly towards the *Xenia*.

★ ★ ★

It was after midnight when Savino returned to the dockside, and his face expressed complete satisfaction when he found that the *Xenia*'s diesel engine was already throbbing softly and that the boat

305

only needed to cast off her moorings to put to sea. He jumped down on to the fishing boat's deck and one by one a small force of five men followed him. They gathered into a group, glancing warily around them and wrinkling their noses at the reek of fish. Savino took a pace forward and called to Panapopolis by name.

And Adrian Cleyton stepped calmly out of the tiny wheelhouse.

Savino's face flinched with alarm and his hand flickered towards his coat pocket. Then he checked the movement as he realized that while the stranger was alone he had five men at his back.

He rasped harshly, "Who are you? Where is the boat's captain?"

Cleyton shrugged expressively and gave an apologetic smile. "You must be Mr. Savino," he observed. "I have a misfortune to explain to you, sir. When you employed my brother to take you to sea tonight you made one big mistake — you paid him in advance. He goes straight to the taverna and now he is very drunk."

Savino's face was no longer handsome as he said suspiciously, "Are you trying to tell me that Panapopolis is drunk — in little more than an hour."

Savino's companions had closed around Cleyton in an ugly circle, but the slim man did not appear to notice and he continued to smile. "That is the sorry truth. Normally my brother drinks only retzina, nothing but retzina. But at the cinema he watches the stars in the American films drink whisky, and tonight, because he has big money, he must try this whisky. And he tries to drink the whisky the way he drinks the wine."

Savino cursed angrily, silenced an interruption from one of his men, and then demanded, "And you say you are Panapopolis's brother?"

Cleyton prayed that Panapopolis had been telling the truth when he had said that he and Savino had never met before and calmly nodded his head. He glanced down at his clothing, a reeking old sweater and a pair of patched trousers he had found in the *Xenia*'s cabin, and added, "I am Hector, and as you can see I am all ready to take my brother's place."

"But I have already paid Panapopolis!"

Cleyton nodded vigorously. "Exactly so. And I must carry out his obligations. It is a matter of honour."

Savino hesitated, then decided abruptly. "All right, it's too late for me to change my plans so you will have to do. Outside the harbour there will be a launch waiting to guide you, and all you have to do is to follow it. Now get moving."

Cleyton beamed widely, thanked him, and then hurried to cast off the mooring ropes. Savino's five men watched him work, and although nothing but cheerful simplicity registered on his face the slim man had already noticed that each man had a trouble-hardened look about him, and that four out of the five were inflicted with a heavy bulge in the right-hand coat pocket. The fifth man carried a medium-sized black suitcase.

Cleyton had never handled a forty-foot fishing boat before, but his trade had called for an extensive training programme that had covered a wide variety of skills, and he knew enough about sailing to clear the dock basin without mishap. And then, exactly as promised, a fast launch nosed out of the night sea to meet them.

Cleyton recognized the launch, and he knew that Christos and Dimitri were probably aboard. He had expected that, but still there was a single, horrible, stomach-gnawing moment when he thought that the launch was coming alongside and that one of the men who knew his face might be transfering to the *Xenia*. Then the launch sped past and Savino snapped at him to keep behind it. Two hours later a small island rose like a blunt, molar tooth from the black sea and Cleyton was told to cut off his engines and let the boat drift. In the same moment he heard the name Kyros murmured by one of the men on deck, and only then did he realize that he was looking at Angelo Valedri's stronghold.

A hundred yards away Christos's launch also drifted silently on the slight swell and Cleyton realized that they were waiting for something to happen, or for some kind of signal.

Nobody spoke, but after a few minutes the man with the suitcase opened it and took out the dismantled parts of a high-powered rifle which he idly began to fit together. Another man produced an automatic and carefully checked the ammunition clip.

Cleyton watched, and the calm way in which they continued to work in front of him made his spine turn cold. He suddenly knew why Savino had agreed to his taking Panapopolis's place with a minimum of argument, for it was clear that something big was soon about to take place and quite obviously no talkative fishing captain was going to be left alive to tell about it.

17

Even Odds

Inside the darkened villa on Kyros Simon Larren slowly descended the wide staircase to the ground floor. In his right hand he held his tiny pencil torch and he directed it downwards to reconnoitre each step before he carefully lowered his foot. Over his left shoulder slumped the unconscious body of Angelo Valedri.

Larren's palms were sweating again and his mouth was just a little bit dry as he moved through the silent building, but there was no sound and no stirring of life to disturb him. He felt that he had probably penetrated all of Valedri's network of defences and that the man would not consider it necessary to post a guard inside the house, but he could not be absolutely sure. He knew that he had to be prepared for the totally

311

unexpected and so he moved with the utmost caution.

He reached the spacious lounge and hesitated for a moment to let his ears strain into the stillness, then he crossed over to the smaller dining-room, paused again, and then moved stealthily into the kitchen. So far all the doors had been open, presumably to let the air circulate through the house, but the door that led down to the cellar was closed. Larren played his torch upon it for a moment and then transferred the torch to his teeth and gently tried the large doorknob. It turned with a slight creak that made him involuntarily grate his teeth upon the torch, and then the heavy door pulled open.

Larren stepped through on to the top step of the stone stairs that led down to the vault-like cellars and attentively closed the door behind him. He saw the large key protruding from the lock and his lips drew back from the metal of the torch in a slow, satisfied smile as the turned it to lock the door.

He moved more swiftly now, no longer

afraid of being heard, taking the torch in his hand again and hurrying down into the cellar. Everything was exactly as he remembered it, and when he switched on the lights at the bottom of the stairs he saw once more the maze of red brick archways and the many racks of dusty wine bottles.

He dropped the torch into his pocket and drew out his automatic in its place before carrying the limp body deeper into the cellar. The desire to have the gun in his hand was mostly habit for he felt reasonably safe now, and he knew from bitter experience that the vaults were soundproof. He looked round for a suitable place to lower his burden and then saw a small pool of spilled red wine on the floor, and some grim sense of justice caused him to deposit Valedri there as he recognized the spot where he had undergone his own interrogation forty-eight hours before.

The ex-assassin for Murder Incorporated looked harmless and almost pathetic now, just a crumpled old man lying in his blue silk pyjamas on the cold flagstones. His temple was bruised and bloodied where Larren's single blow bad broken the skin and his dark face looked much older than the last time that Larren had seen it. His eyes and his mouth were closed and he was breathing sluggishly through the nose.

Larren's mouth had resumed its normal, unsmiling hardness and his grey-green eyes were blank of all sympathy as he looked down at his prisoner. He was thinking of the red death; of the slow-creeping paralysis, of the ugly red rash on a child's face, and of the ever-climbing total of corpses that the scourge left in its wake: and he knew that Angelo Valedri was still as coldly vicious and as utterly evil as he had been in his youth; more so, for he no longer murdered in ones or twos, but in scores and hundreds.

Calmly Larren took another set of cords from his pocket and swiftly and efficiently tied Valedri's wrists and ankles together. He did not bother with a gag for he intended that Valedri should talk, and reaching for a full wine bottle from the nearest rack he wrenched out the cork with a twisting pull of his teeth and tipped its contents full into the old man's face.

Valedri choked and twisted his face away as the red wine ran over his chin and into his hair, flooding up his nostrils and filling his ears. The wine drained away to form a pool below his head but still he remained unconscious. Larren extracted the cork from a second bottle and repeated the procedure, and on the fourth try Valedri choked and gasped his way back to life.

Larren watched as the man gagged helplessly, twisting his head to shake off the wine and then wincing with pain as the movement brought stabs of agony from his bloodied temple. Valedri's eyes were still clamped shut, but when he was able to open them Larren spoke to him softly.

"Remember me, Valedri?"

Valedri blinked up at him and his body writhed in restrained fury as he made an enraged effort to break free. When he realized that he had no hope of succeeding his body relaxed into violent trembling and he said savagely,

315

"You'll die for this, Larren. You'll die so goddamned slow that you'll beg and scream for death long before it's over."

Larren's expression didn't change. He said flatly, "I don't think so, Valedri. You know as well as I do that this cellar is soundproof. Nobody is going to disturb us down here."

Valedri laughed harshly. "That may be so — but you've got to get out of here, Larren, and I promise you that you'll never get off Kyros alive."

Larren smiled and said pointedly, "I got here alive. I now know where the trip wire is and I've already cleared one section of the cliffs of your patrolling guard and dog teams. There's no reason why I shouldn't get back the same way."

Valedri cursed foully, and then demanded, "All right, Larren. What is it you want?"

"It's quite simple." Larren made it sound as though it was. "All I want are the samples of the Ameytheline anti-dote that your son discovered before he was killed. I know that you must have them somewhere in the villa."

Valedri's swarthy face twisted into another spasm of harsh laughter. "And you think that all you have to do is ask for them! Larren, you're a fool. You'll never find out where those samples are hidden before dawn. And at dawn I'm going to be missed and Bruno and the others are going to start searching for me. When that happens you won't have a hope in hell of getting away."

Larren remained silent for a moment, and the sardonic glitter in his grey-green eyes slowly killed the small trace of laughter that still showed on Valedri's face. A small flicker of fear passed across the old man's dark face and he flinched beneath that cold, appraising gaze.

Then Larren said softly, "I think you'll talk before then, Valedri. I think you'll be only too pleased to tell me where those antidote samples are."

Then he reached into his pocket and drew out the small flat box that he had brought all the way from London. He opened it with careful fingers and showed Valedri the contents. The inside of the box was softly lined with blue velvet and

317

contained four tiny glass capsules and a hypodermic syringe fitted with a long, slender needle.

"Recognize them?" Larren asked, his voice still soft and caressing. "The capsules contain Ameytheline, Valedri. A difficult drug to get hold of now that it has proved itself a killer. But a very useful drug to have."

Valedri's throat moved helplessly as he swallowed a mouthful of air, but he said nothing.

Larren delicately placed the box on top of the rack of wine bottles where it could not fall off and then selected one of the tiny capsules. He removed the minute cap and held the capsule in front of Valedri as he dipped the needle of the hypodermic inside and slowly filled the syringe.

Valedri said hoarsely, "This won't get you anywhere, Larren."

"No?" Larren spoke the word inquiringly, and then he dropped one knee heavily on to Valedri's chest. Valedri struggled desperately but Larren's weight pinned him down. The old man cursed and screeched as Larren tore his pyjama jacket from one shoulder, ripping the material away down the length of his arm. Deftly Larren gripped the bared arm at the elbow and then he thrust the needle of the hypodermic deep into the yielding flesh and depressed the plunger.

Larren held the needle in place until the syringe had emptied, and then he slowly straightened himself up. Valedri lay at his feet, his mouth twisted and his dark face ashen, his body still squirming feebly. The old man finally relaxed slightly and hissed defiantly.

"Ameytheline's killer effects are long delayed, Larren. Are you going to wait around for a year or two until paralysis sets in?"

Larren shook his head. "You don't seem to have realized," he said conversationally, "but the effects are only long delayed when the drug is administered in the proper quantities. On the other hand an overdose can be immediately fatal. Now if I were a doctor, or a chemist, I would know how many of these little capsules constitute an ordinary dose, but unfortunately I happen to be

319

somewhat ignorant on the subject, and the only way to find out is by trial and error." Still smiling he broke the cap of a second capsule and began to refill the hypodermic.

Valedri's face began to show the first tiny globules of perspiration as he watched Larren's hands preparing the second injection. His mouth began to twitch and he again gulped down a large mouthful of air.

"I'll kill you for this, Larren!" He yelled suddenly. "I'll kill you! I'll tear your crummy — "

Larren dropped on to his chest again and slammed the man's mouth shut by thrusting the heel of his hand hard against the underside of his chin. Valedri's bound legs kicked and threshed about the cellar floor but still he was helpless in the tall Britisher's grasp. His head was pushed back and the slender needle pierced the side of his neck to pump another full dose of the killer drug into his bloodstream.

When Larren rose to his feet again he was still smiling, and his voice still retained its note of conversational amicability.

"I think that should prove fatal," he murmured. "But we had better use another capsule just to be sure."

He selected a third of the tiny glass containers and again made sure that Valedri could see every move as he filled the hypodermic once more. When the capsule was empty he casually flicked it away across the cellar and then held the syringe before his eyes as though to examine it more closely. Without looking at Valedri he said idly, "Of course, you do realize the purpose of this experiment? The idea is to try and find out whether the antidote prepared to combat the long delayed effects of this nasty little drug can also counteract the effects of a lethal overdose." He glanced down and allowed himself the barest suspicion of a smile. "What do you think, Valedri?"

A combination of fear and rage twisted Valedri's answer into a meaningless snarl of obscenities.

Larren shrugged and again knelt on the old man's stomach, holding the frenzied

321

body fast to the flagstones as he ripped the blue silk pyjamas down from the waist. He gripped Valedri's left leg at the knee and held it still as he aimed the slender needle at the blue vein that ran along the thigh.

Valedri screamed as the needle sank home, screeching and yelling Bruno's name over and over again in deranged fury.

Larren stood up with the empty syringe and regarded him sadly. "It's no use, Valedri. The cellar is soundproof — remember? This was where you brought me so that Carla shouldn't hear my screams."

Valedri's mouthings died off into sobbing curses. "Blast you, Larren. You'll never find that antidote. Never!"

"If I don't find it then you're a dead man."

"No, Larren," he raged defiantly. "I can last until dawn — and at dawn Bruno will come looking for me. You'll be the one to die — and Bruno can give me a shot of the antidote."

Larren shook his head. "Dawn will be

too late, you will probably be dead by then. And even if you're not I still doubt if the antidote will help you at that stage. In fact, in your case, with such a large overdose I can't be sure that the antidote will help you at all. I should say that your chances of living, even with a shot of the antidote, are no more than fifty-fifty. That's even odds, Valedri, and those odds are shortening with every minute you waste."

Valedri swore foully. The sweat lay on his face in a thousand and glistening droplets and his complexion had gone the colour of dirty chalk.

Larren sighed and prepared the fourth injection.

When it was ready he glanced down and asked gently, "Where is the Ameytheline antidote?"

Valedri's mouth was closed tight and he seemed unable to speak. But his eyes still radiated defiance as well as fear and he shook his head.

Larren held him down and again emptied the hypodermic into his thigh. Somehow Valedri refrained from any further useless struggle, and when Larren rose to his feet the old man lay like a wax dummy and only his hate-filled eyes were alive.

Larren said quietly, "Now we wait, Valedri. With that amount of drug circulating through your bloodstream you can't possibly have much time. The only chance you have is to tell me where to find that antidote and I promise you that you'll get one shot before I leave. You can save yourself — or you can die. It's up to you."

Valedri's bloodless lips moved once.

"You can go to hell, Larren. You can go to bloody hell!"

* * *

An hour passed, and then another, and Simon Larren waited and watched as the drug slowly but surely killed the old man at his feet. Valedri's face was completely bloodless and drenched with sweat, and after the first hour both his legs had become numb with paralysis. His breathing was a hoarse, desperate sound that grated horribly in his throat and occasionally his shoulders would twitch and a shudder would run through the upper half of his body. By the end of the second hour his left arm, the one in which Larren had made the first injection, was also paralysed, and it was clear that soon the slow-creeping numbness would reach his heart.

Larren knew that if Valedri did not talk now he would never talk at all, and he knelt beside the old man and spoke his name softly.

Valedri's eyes opened, staring, but dulling with the approach of death. His mouth worked helplessly but no sound came out.

Larren said quietly, "You're leaving it too late, Valedri. You can see now that you'll never last until dawn. The only chance you have lies with me."

Valedri tried to speak but nothing but unintelligible croaks escaped through his bloodless lips, and Larren suddenly realized in horror that the injection in the neck had frozen the man's vocal cords.

He said desperately, "You've got to

talk, Valedri. In another hour you'll be dead."

Valedri's mouth moved again, uttering harsh rattling sounds that he could not form into words. And then Larren recognized the syllables of one repeated effort.

"Wall?" He encouraged. "You're trying to say something about a wall."

Valedri nodded weakly but could say nothing more. The sounds straining in his throat were more animal than human.

Larren thought hard and then demanded, "A wall safe, is that it?" Valedri nodded and again Larren's thoughts raced. Where would the man keep a wall safe containing anything as valuable as the antidote? He could only think of one answer and asked swiftly. "The bedroom? Is it in your bedroom?"

Again Valedri could only nod his head feebly.

Larren knew that the man was beaten, but now that he could no longer talk it seemed that he had won after all, even though unwillingly. He knew there was no hope of getting an answer to the all important question that followed, but he had to try.

"Where is the key, Valedri? Where is the key?"

Valedri's answer sounded like a death rattle and his throat worked helplessly.

For a moment Larren felt the bitter taste of defeat fouling the back of his mouth, and then a last-minute idea flickered through his brain. He swiftly pulled out his knife and cut the old man's wrists free, and then he pulled a notebook and a pen from his pocket and pushed the pen into the man's right hand. Hope surged through him as he saw that the dying gangster still had enough strength in that one hand to hold the pen.

He lifted the hand holding the pen on to Valedri's chest and steadied it at the elbow. With his other hand he held the book in front of the pen so that Valedri could see it.

"There's a chance that the antidote can still save you," he urged. "Tell me where to find the key?"

Very slowly, very feebly, the hand holding the pen moved. Larren watched the word appear on the white paper, a scrawling, wavering line that was almost unreadable. And then as the fingers relaxed and the pen fell away he recognized it — and the idea seemed so ludicrous that he almost laughed.

"The pillow," he read aloud. "The key is under your pillow!"

Valedri nodded, and closed his eyes.

Larren left him and ran swiftly across the cellar, shutting off the lights and hurrying up the stone steps. His pencil torch was back in his hand and he played it on the big key in the cellar door as he unlocked it and slipped back into the ground-floor kitchen. He knew that it was nearer to dawn than he had dared to admit to Valedri, and that he did not have much time if he was going to escape from Kyros while it was still dark. Already the blackness was not quite so absolute, and although he still moved with stealth and the utmost caution he wasted no time in returning to Valedri's bedroom.

He felt under the pillow of the empty bed and smiled softly to himself as his fingers closed over the cold metal of a small key. Quickly he played the torch beam around the walls in search of the safe, and after two minutes he found it behind a framed picture of a reclining nude by a water-fall. The key opened the safe with well-oiled ease and the small square door swung back without a sound. Larren hardly dared to breathe as he shone his torch into the interior.

There, nestling like fragile eggs in a nest, were three small glass phials together with a sheaf of notebooks. Larren opened the top book, and although the jumble of figures and symbols inside meant nothing to him he was fairly sure that these had to be the missing notes containing Paolo Castel's formula for the stolen antidote. Swiftly Larren stuffed the notebooks into the inside pocket of his jacket, and then, using more care, he transferred the three phials to the breast pocket of his shirt and buttoned down the flap. Then he closed up the safe and made his way swiftly and silently back to the cellar.

Larren had been tempted to make his escape immediately, but he knew that it was just possible that he had been fooled and that the phials in his pocket could be dummies, and he had to be absolutely sure that he was carrying the right formula before he left the island.

He found that Valedri was still alive, and the man's eyes flickered open as he approached.

Larren showed him one of the phials, and the desperate light of hope that suddenly appeared in that dark, dying gaze told Larren that the phials really did contain the vital antidote. Valedri grunted helplessly and his feverish stare searched around until Larren picked up the syringe he had left in its case on top of the bottles and held it so that the man could see. Valedri's eyes were begging, and even though Larren knew that it must be too late some strange combination of conscience and the reluctance to break his word caused him to fill the hypodermic from one of the phials.

He gave Valedri the last injection in the vein in the thigh where he thought it might do the most good, but when he stood up Valedri lay perfectly still and his eyes were closed.

The injection had killed him.

Larren stared down impassively at the dead shell of the man who had once terrorized the underworld of Chicago as a hired killer for Murder Incorporated; the man who had tried to blackmail the Government of England from his island stronghold, and the man whose greed had caused a plague and a thousand deaths.

Then very calmly he said, "I warned you, Valedri. All you had was even odds."

★ ★ ★

A few minutes later Larren left the cellar for the last time, passing through the kitchen and dining-room and entering the lounge. Grey streaks of light were beginning to penetrate the villa now and he knew that he could not count on much more than an hour to reach his launch before the alarm was raised. However, he felt that an hour should be plenty and he was not unduly worried as he turned towards the stairs. He meant to leave by the second-floor balcony and retrace his steps exactly as he had come in, for he reasoned that the route he already knew was less likely to provide any unexpected snags.

Then an unexpected snag arose right in front of him as a shadowy figure stepped out of the darkness at the foot of the staircase and said savagely, "Don't move, Simon. If you raise that gun or take another step I'll kill you."

Larren froze. The voice was Carla's and she moved a pace closer, the automatic in her hand holding rock steady in the dim grey light. Slowly Larren let his own automatic fall to the carpet at his feet.

Carla said coldly, "I found Antonella, Simon. I went to her room and found her all tied up, and she told me that you were responsible." Her dark eyes were furious and the automatic did tremble slightly now. "You used me, Simon. You tricked me into bringing you here to Kyros and made a fool of me. You made a fool out of me!" Her voice rose hysterically and the gun shuddered violently in her hand. "I'm going to kill you for that, Simon.

I'm going to kill you!"

She raised the automatic to fire — and in that same moment a shattering outburst of gun shots sounded from the direction of the beach.

18

All Roads Lead to Kyros

Carla Valedri hesitated with her finger still taking up the first pressure on the trigger of the automatic. The blind rage in her eyes seemed to be shocked into stillness, and very slowly it was replaced by alarm as she listened to the rattle of gunfire from the beach. Her lovely body suddenly trembled and her full breasts strained against the loose blouse she was wearing. For a moment the sharp, rising taste of fear caught in her throat and swamped the anger and emotions of a few seconds before. Her tone was empty of hysteria and she spoke with a note of wavering uncertainty.

"What is it, Simon? What's happening?"

Larren could recognize the spitting bark of several automatics and the sharp, isolated crack of a single rifle, but apart from that he had no idea of what was going on. His brain cells practically tumbled over one another as he sought desperately for some means of turning the interruption to his advantage and he blurted desperately, "There's no time to explain, Carla. But that's why I'm here. You and I have got to get away — quickly."

He stepped forward appealingly but the automatic jabbed at his chest and brought him to an abrupt halt. Carla was searching his face with wide, bewildered eyes and it was plain that her thoughts had been scattered beyond immediate recall.

"My father," she faltered. "Antonella said you went looking for my father."

Larren fumbled for a fraction of a second and then told the first lie that jumped into his mind. "Your father and I have made a deal." He could hear the shouts and curses from above as the rest of Valedri's household came to life and he went on insistently. "There's no time to explain the details now, but part of the deal was that I should get you out of here. Now put that gun down and come on."

"I don't believe you." There was still doubt in her tone but it was beginning to fade, and her former mood was returning as she realized that the gunfire was not yet close to the villa. She said again, "You played me for a fool. For that I ought to kill you."

Larren ignored the automatic that still bored its snout hard against his chest and clamped both hands on her shoulders. His heart was pounding horribly and his stomach seemed to be whirling like a slow spinning top, but his voice was hard and commanding as he said, "I don't think you could do it, Carla. Even if I was an enemy of your father's, I still don't think you could do it." Despite the gun between them his mouth was only inches from her own and he finished up harshly. "You're too damned man-hungry, Carla. Just too damned man-hungry." And then he kissed her hard on the mouth.

Carla Valedri made one half flinching effort to draw back, but the cruel touch of his lips drained the will-power from her body and she moaned weakly as she parted her own lips to meet him. The automatic slowly folded between them, crushed flat between the soft mounds of her breasts and the hard muscles of his chest as she drew her hand away. Then her arms moved round his waist and her hands clutched at his shoulders.

"Simon, I love you." She breathed the words into his mouth as they kissed, her lips hungry and ever-searching. "I need you, Simon. Take me away — please."

"Do you trust me now?" he demanded roughly.

Her answer was muffled but unmistakable, and he knew that for the moment, and for any other moment when their bodies made contact, she would be a puppet in his hands. The demands of her body made the hapless Carla a slave to any man who could satisfy her craving, and helped her to shut her mind to any other thoughts or loyalties.

Another series of shots sounded from the beach and from above came the clatter of footsteps in the corridor outside the bedrooms. A door slammed and the bawling voice of Bruno sounded above the mêlée. Larren swiftly scooped one hand under the back of Carla's thighs and lifted her into his arms as he turned and dived back into the safety of the dining-room.

Seconds later Bruno came running down the stairs with a gun in his hand and three men at his heels, and all four crashed across the lounge, through the main doors and out into the pale grey dawn.

Larren lowered Carla to the floor and disentangled himself from her arms. "We can do that later," he promised. "Right now I've got to get you off this island."

He had her automatic in his hand now and with his left arm about her waist he hustled her across the lounge and warily surveyed the scene on the distant beach through the open door.

A launch had just landed at the small jetty and three men were frantically running away from it, heading towards the villa over the soft sand. Larren recognized two of them as Valedri's hirelings, but the man in the middle, an older, slower man who was being half dragged by his companions was a complete stranger. Further along the beach a second launch had landed and Larren recognized it as the craft that belonged to Christos; and seconds later he saw the tall Greek leading Dimitri and a third man in a desperate effort to cut off the running trio who were trying to reach the house. A few yards beyond Christos's launch a forty-foot fishing boat was just on the point of landing and in its bows stood the man with the single rifle. Another small party was scrambling over the fishing boat's side and running up the beach, and Larren thought he recognized Savino in the lead. Nearer to the villa Bruno was leading his small force to join up with a small group of four men who were already crouching at the top of the beach and providing covering fire for the first three running men.

As Larren watched the three fugitives reached the first line of defenders and threw themselves down beside them. This first line obviously consisted of the patrolling guards who roamed the island, for two of them still held straining wolfhounds, similar to the one Larren had killed, on a short leash. The moment the fugitives were momentarily safe the guard dogs were released and sent charging savagely at Christos and his two companions.

The tall, blue-jawed Greek dropped to one knee in the sand, coolly aimed his automatic, and neatly shot the first dog through the chest as it leapt at him. The second brute carried the less fortunate Dimitri to the ground, but the third man fired two bullets into its spine before the tearing jaws could do too much damage. Christos helped his lieutenant up and all three retreated to wait for the reinforcements from the fishing boat.

By now Bruno's party had joined up with the original guards and soon a violent gun battle was taking place. Larren could see Bruno rapping orders to his men who immediately began to spread out in a determined defensive line; and then one man broke away from the group and began to hustle the old man who had been one of the three fugitives towards the safety of the villa.

Quite suddenly Larren realized who the old man was.

He could only be Andromavitch.

The explanation to the unexpected battle on the beach became suddenly plain. Andromavitch had either been kidnapped, or else persuaded to surrender himself to Valedri's thugs, and somehow Christos had learned that the scientist was due to arrive on Kyros at dawn this morning. Consequently Christos and his so-called crime syndicate were moving in to scoop both Andromavitch and the Ameytheline antidote in one savage swoop. However, Larren could not visualize an expert like Christos intending such a crazy mix-up as the one that was taking place now, and he guessed that somewhere the tall Greek's plans had gone astray. More probably they had attempted a pirate raid on the launch carrying Andromavitch while it was still out on the Aegean, but somehow they had blundered and the launch had reached the shore to give the alarm.

Larren felt a quiver of excitement as he realized that his surmise must be correct, but the only answer that he could not reason out was how could Christos have known so much about Valedri's plans. Then Carla, who had moved closer beside him in the doorway, supplied the final answer. She touched his arm and said sharply, "Look, Simon. Look over there!"

Larren followed the direction of her pointing finger and a hundred yards to their left he saw a slim figure in black jeans and a yellow blouse crouching almost double and running fast through the rocks and scrub. It could only be Antonella, and she was heading away from the house on a course that would take her around the battle in a wide looping circle to join up with Christos and the invaders on the beach.

"It's Antonella!" Carla exclaimed in surprise. "But what on earth does she think she's doing?"

Larren said briefly, "Haven't you recognized your friends Christos and Savino down there on the beach? The men who tried to kidnap you. Antonella is running to join them and it's pretty obvious that she must have been betraying your father." He saw an opening for another lie and added, "That's probably why she tried to give you the untrue impression that I meant your father harm when you released her."

"The bitch!" Carla burst out vehemently. "The rotten, lying little bitch!"

Then abruptly the mention of Valedri jogged her memory and she stared up at Larren's face. "My father! Where — where is he?"

Larren crushed his conscience with a savage effort and said, "Don't worry — he's all right. He stayed behind to destroy some papers and things that he doesn't want to fall into Savino's hands. He has his own escape route planned when he's ready, but he didn't have time to give me the full details. Meanwhile he's entrusted me to get you away from Kyros."

"I — I still don't understand," she protested feebly.

Larren smiled. "Of course not, but right now just trust me until we're safely back in Athens. Will you do that?"

She hesitated, and then nodded slowly.

"Good." Larren gave her shoulder an encouraging squeeze. Out of one corner of his eye he could see that Andromavitch and his single guard were half-way towards the villa and he went on swiftly, "Do you think you can find me a good length of rope. I want something that will reach from the cliff tops to the sea so it must be at least one hundred feet long."

She looked dubious. "I can find two fifty-foot coils."

"Get them," Larren ordered. "And then take them up to that high pinnacle of rock on the cliffs that you pointed out to me when we first came here — the place you called the sanctuary of Poseidon. I've got a launch waiting below the cliffs there and that's the way we're making our escape. Hurry now, and I'll catch you up in a few minutes."

Carla looked dazed. "But, Simon, what about — "

Larren seized her shoulders, kissed her violently, and pushed her away. "Get going, Carla. There isn't time for any questions."

A renewed burst of gunfire from the beach hammered home the truth of his words and without any further argument she turned and ran off through the back of the house. Larren heaved a sigh of relief as she disappeared, and then turned his attention back to the two men who were now hurrying over the last fifty yards to the doorway where he stood.

Grimly he stepped to one side and waited, slipping Carla's automatic into his pocket and drawing his sheath knife in its place. He knew that the tiny phials of liquid in his breast pocket were priceless, but so was the knowledge stored inside the brain of the approaching nuclear scientist and he could not leave the man to fall into Christos's hands.

The sound of gun shots still crackled on the beach and Larren wondered how much time he would have before the battle ended and the victors realized that the prizes were being snatched from under their noses. He knew that if the fighting came to a swift close then his own chances of escaping would be slim indeed, and he earnestly hoped that both contesting sides would dig in their heels and fight to the bitter end.

His palms were sweating again and he carefully smoothed them down his thighs to remove the moisture, and then he heard the footfalls of Andromavitch and his companion as they scraped on the first of the wide steps before the doorway. Two shadows fell through the entrance and Larren's muscles tensed, then the first man was entering the villa.

Larren held back as he realized that this man was old and stooping, and he prayed that Andromavitch would not look round and reveal his presence before the second man stepped inside. Then the other man appeared, and even without the smart white suit Larren recognized him as the manservant who had helped Bruno and Valedri to conduct his interrogation. His grey-green eyes gleamed with pleasure as he stepped silently forward, and his left hand closed over the manservant's mouth and jerked him backwards. The knife flashed once before blood dulled the silver of the blade, and the dead man was lowered slowly to the ground with his last breath still gurgling slightly in his gashed throat.

Andromavitch turned clumsily at the noise and his lined face contorted with horror. He took a staggering step back and raised his hands in a wild gesture of self-protection.

Larren said swiftly. "Everything's all right, Professor. I'm an agent for British Intelligence, and from now on you're in my care."

The words did nothing to reassure the scientist, and if Larren could have seen the picture he presented he would have realized why. He looked far more villainous than any of the struggling desperadoes on the beach; his clothing was still wet and crumpled, and plastered with sand where he had wriggled up to the villa; his face was a hard, unsmiling frame for eyes that could well have been transplanted from a hunting Jaguar; and tiny drops of red still drained from the sheath knife in his right hand.

Larren went on. "I take it that you are

Professor Andromavitch?"

The old man had lowered his hands but he was still unable to speak, and he simply nodded his head. He had a fine shock of bright ginger-red hair that helped to conceal his true age, and despite his present air of helplessness he was a large-boned man who looked as though he would still be strong and active once he had recovered his balance. His hands looked big and clumsy for a scientist, but his broad, deeply-furrowed forehead was more in relation to his exceptional brain power. His brows were ginger and bushy and the eyes beneath them had a peculiar penetrating quality, but apart from that their colour was undefinable. There was something vaguely disturbing about those eyes, but Larren couldn't quite place what it was.

Then Andromavitch recovered the power of speech and declared hoarsely, "You — you just murdered that man. You *butchered* him!"

Larren picked up a cushion from a nearby chair, cleaned his knife, and calmly returned it to its hidden sheath that was reached through the inside pocket of his jacket. "It was necessary," he explained simply. "And now you've got to trust me, Professor. I have no means of identification, but I assure you that I am employed, although somewhat indirectly, by the British Government. And I do have a launch ready to get you away from here."

Andromavitch stiffened his shoulders and said slowly, "And what if I refuse to go?"

Larren showed him one of the glass phials from his shirt pocket and answered grimly, "There's no need for you to refuse, Professor. This is the antidote to the red death that Angelo Valedri offered in exchange for your knowledge. And now let's stop wasting time and get out of here while the rest of the party is still squabbling."

The sight of the tiny glass container that Larren held between his finger and thumb robbed Andromavitch of any further argument. He watched as Larren replaced the antidote sample and rebuttoned the flap over his shirt pocket, and he made no resistance as Larren extracted his automatic from his coat pocket and then took him by the shoulder and hustled him out of the villa.

The pitched battle on the beach was still in full swing, but Bruno and the island's defenders seemed to be getting the worst of it. Two of their number now lay motionless on the sand, and a third was twisting helplessly and clutching a shattered knee-cap. The remainder were firing more frequently and far more haphazardly than Christos and his party, who were now swelled by the group from the fishing boat, and Larren saw that it would not be long before they ran out of ammunition.

Larren realized that Christos and Savino must eventually take the island, for although Bruno was an ugly and dangerous man, he was still a child compared to the tall, blue-jawed Greek. Besides which, the fact that Valedri had not appeared and must seem to have deserted them would soon rob Bruno's companions of the heart to fight. For their kind would not continue to risk death to defend a leader who would not stand beside them.

Grimly Larren turned away from the beach and hurried Andromavitch along the side of the villa. A grove of olive trees offered a small patch of cover and he sprinted across the intervening space with Andromavitch protesting hoarsely beside him. He was certain from the reckless way in which Bruno and his men had dashed down to the beach that the high voltage trip wire must have been switched off at dawn, and he wasted no time as he dodged through the gnarled trunks of the olives. The ground beyond rose steeply and was covered with rocks and scrub, and Larren dragged the old man up the slope.

Half-way up the slope Carla suddenly rose from behind a clump of bramble-strangled rocks and ran to meet him.

"Simon. Simon, you took so long. Where — ? Who — ?"

"The rope," Larren said savagely. "Did you get the rope?"

351

She nodded. "Yes. It's behind the rocks. But — "

"There's no time for buts!"

Larren pushed past her and heaved a sigh of relief as he saw the two heavy coils of rope lying in the grass behind the rocks. He stooped and hoisted a coil on to each shoulder and then turned back to his companions.

"Come on, we've — "

He realized abruptly that the shooting had stopped, and that both Carla and Andromavitch were staring down to the beach over the tops of the olive trees.

Bruno's party had surrendered and Christos's men were efficiently rounding them up and herding them into a small guarded circle near the jetty. Further along the beach stood Christos himself, his automatic held loosely at his side. Antonella was with him, her vivid yellow blouse easily distinguishable, and she was pointing up to the three fugitives up in the rocks.

Christos suddenly left her and raced up the beach. He yelled orders as he went and both Savino and Dimitri turned from

352

the task of rounding up the prisoners and followed him. Dimitri paused only long enough to snatch the single rifle from its owner and then all three were in furious pursuit.

19

At the Sanctuary of Poseidon

Larren knew that only speed could save them now, and grabbing Andromavitch by the shoulder he mercilessly propelled the complaining Russian up the steep slope. Carla stumbled desperately at his heels, too frightened and too breathless to worry him with any further questions and dragging at the elbow of his jacket as she struggled to keep pace. The two coils of rope were hampering Larren's progress and he uttered a violent oath as one of them slipped down to catch in the crook of his arm. He had to falter a moment to hoist the rope back into place and at the same time risked a swift glance behind him. He saw that Christos and Savino had both reached the grassy slope leading up to the villa in its bowl in the hills below; but Dimitri had stopped to kneel in the sand of the beach and was coolly squinting through the sites of his raised rifle.

Larren hurled himself flat, pulling both Carla and Andromavitch down to the earth with him as the ringing crack of the rifle whined through the still morning air. The bullet sang a rustling course through the leaves of a small bush directly ahead of them, and buried itself into the earth beyond.

Larren ignored the roaring anger of Andromavitch and the half sobbing, half whimpering sounds that came from the terrified Carla, twisting his body round to look back to the beach. Dimitri had lowered his rifle as he stared towards them, but when he realized that he had missed after all he raised the weapon again.

Larren's face tightened with savage, helpless fury as he realized that he was trapped. All that Dimitri had to do was to pin them down with the rifle until Christos and Savino could close in for the kill.

Then an angry yell from Christos, who had stopped at the sound of the shot, made Dimitri reluctantly lower the rifle. Larren watched as Dimitri rose to his feet and started running again with the rifle held low by his side and realized that he still had a chance.

Christos was obviously afraid of hitting Andromavitch, and so he had ordered his lieutenant to hold his fire.

Swiftly Larren scrambled to his feet, but instead of pushing Andromavitch ahead of him he took the lead himself and hauled the scientist in his wake as a shield. It was not the heroic thing to do, but Larren was interested only in saving all their lives and not in heroics. He knew that if he died then both Andromavitch and the Ameytheline antidote would be lost, and now that he knew that Christos did not want to hit the old man then it was common sense to make him bring up the rear.

Carla still ran at his side, sobbing painfully for breath and clutching at his arm. Her lovely, raven-black hair was streaming wild and loose over her shoulders and her firm breasts swelled violently against her blouse as she strained her lungs for air. She was past logical reasoning now and hung blindly on to Larren's arm.

Andromavitch still protested as he manipulated his clumsy body up the hill, but since that single rifle shot that had sent them all cowering to the ground his protests had lost strength and he was now almost as eager as Larren to keep going.

They reached the top of the slope and then the beach and the villa were hidden behind its crest as they started down a slight incline. The ground ahead of them soon rose again and continued in a series of rolls and hollows, gradually rising for almost half a mile to the point where it dropped sheer to the sea. Ahead they could see the top of the rocky spire that marked the sanctuary of Poseidon, but the uneven terrain they had to cross was a maze of tumbled, grey-white rocks, bramble patches and low scrub bushes. Christos and his two companions were now out of sight behind them, but Larren allowed his charges no respite.

The two coils of rope hung heavily on

Larren's shoulders and hampered all his movements, and every few minutes one of them would insistently slip down to lodge in the crook of his elbow and have to be hoisted into place again. Finally the awkwardness of trying to do four jobs with two hands caused him to stop and transfer both coils to his right shoulder. Then he reluctantly dropped his automatic into his pocket and held on to both ropes with one hand while he towed Andromavitch with the other. He would have preferred to keep the gun in his hand and release Andromavitch, but every time he relaxed his grip on the other's arm the old man lagged feebly behind and Larren could not afford to let him rest. Carla still held on to his coat sleeve.

The sun was still very low in the eastern sky, but Larren found himself sweating hard from the exertion of running. He knew from the hoarse sounds of their breathing that his two companions were worse off than he was and he began to wonder whether he could get them to safety before they collapsed. It was beginning to seem very doubtful.

There was no sign of their pursuers now, and it was almost possible to believe that the three men behind them had given up and turned back. But Larren was sure that a man like Christos would never give up, and that the tall Greek was still trying to catch them through the rocks and hollows that covered this higher part of the island.

So they ran on, scrambling and leaping over the rough ground while fear flailed behind them like an invisible whip. Andromavitch was gradually slowing up, despite Larren's efforts and Carla was half crying from the slashing brambles that had cut and marred the soft white flesh of her bare legs below her flying skirt. Larren knew that he had had something like a quarter mile lead at the start, but he had so many disadvantages that by now Christos must be closing the gap.

The seemingly unattainable spire of rock ahead of them was fast becoming blurred in Larren's vision and his heart was drumming wildly beneath his ribs. And then, just when he was beginning to believe that the spire was

359

a mirage and could only exist in his fevered imagination, he found that he was stumbling to a halt directly in front of it. The pinnacle rose into a point some eighteen feet high, like a crude spearhead carefully balanced in an upright position by some legendary stone-age giant centuries ago. A flight of steep, shallow steps had been cut into the face of the rock, and a few yards behind it the cliff tops came to an abrupt halt with the Aegean gleaming like a vast mirror of silvery blue beyond.

Larren released his hold on Andromavitch and both his charges sank weakly to the ground, Carla falling animal-like to her hands and knees while the scientist managed a more dignified sitting position and slumped forward with his head in his hands. Larren badly wanted to fall down beside them but he remained upright to take in the details of the sanctuary. It was merely a deep hollow in an area of large tumbles of boulders, and only the unnatural spear of weathered rock in front of him separated it from any of the other dips and hollows they had passed. However, that regal pinnacle was commanding enough in its own right, and it was not hard to appreciate why the ancient inhabitants of Kyros had attributed a religious significance to it and named it a sanctuary to the sea god.

Swiftly Larren moved past it to the cliff edge and searched the sea below for his launch. The boat was still there, almost directly below, and for the first time since he had seen Antonella betraying him to Christos he began to feel that he really had a chance. He slipped the two coils of rope from his shoulder and knelt on the cliff top to knot them together into one continuous one-hundred-foot length. Then he lashed one end securely about the most convenient boulder and hurled the rest of the rope out into space; it uncoiled with a slow twisting movement and slapped against the rock face to dangle some fifteen feet short of the sea. Larren decided grimly that they would have to drop the last stretch and then swim out to the launch which was twenty yards or so out from the base of the cliffs.

He turned back to his companions and pulled them both to their feet. They were still staggering slightly as he hustled them over to the cliff edge, and when they saw the descent that awaited them they both stared unbelievably. Carla was too stunned to speak but Andromavitch gasped despairingly.

"But I can never climb down there! It is madness — utter madness!"

Larren realized bitterly that the old man was right. He and Carla would never climb down the rope, especially in their present, shattered condition; they would have to be lowered.

Savagely he began hauling the rope back on to the cliff top.

He said curtly. "I'll tie the rope round your waist and let you down slowly. When you get to the bottom you'll have to release yourself and drop into the sea, then swim to the launch. Understood?"

Andromavitch said wildly, "No! It is too dangerous. I refuse!"

Larren turned to face him, practically

snarling with anger. "You've no bloody choice," he rasped. "This is the only way out."

The muscles of the Russian's fleshy face seemed to vibrate with anger and his lips pursed into a derisive snort. "For you maybe. But I do not think those men were firing at me — and I noticed that you took great care to use me as a shield." His voice gained a note of arrogance as he added abruptly, "So far I have only your word that you are a British agent. How can I know that I will not be safer with your enemies?"

Larren reached the end of the rope and stepped back from the cliff edge. His mouth was set hard and his eyes gleamed like the reflection of grey-green flames on highly-polished steel. He said flatly, "Right now there's no time to argue, Professor. I'm going to tie this round your waist and drop you over the edge no matter what you think. So you might just as well accept the idea."

Andromavitch backed away and the arrogance drained from his face. "Wait," he blurted. "You do not understand.

I — I cannot swim. If you lower me into the sea I shall drown. I could never reach your launch."

Larren stopped in his tracks and felt as though the cliff had suddenly fallen away from under his feet. For a moment he flatly rejected the statement and demanded stupidly, "What the hell do you mean? A child could swim those few strokes!"

Andromavitch began to lose his temper and shouted angrily.

"I cannot help that. I cannot swim even one stroke and I am not going to be dropped into the sea." His face had flushed hotly beneath his thick red hair and for a moment he looked like any bad-tempered old man arguing with someone who was many years his junior.

Larren glared at him and felt an abrupt sensation of deep hatred towards the stubborn Russian, but before they could quarrel any further the vicious, waspish bark of an automatic violated the silence of the sanctuary.

Larren did not know how close the actual bullet had come for it vanished into space above the sea, but he instinctively pulled Carla and Andromavitch down behind the tall spear of rugged rock and clawed his automatic out of his pocket. Sheer necessity killed off his rising fury towards the ageing scientist and he said flatly, "It hardly matters now — our friends have caught up with us."

As he spoke he knew that he was virtually finished, for he could hardly hope to come out victorious against three war-trained professionals. Even if he had been facing Christos alone he would have been doubtful of the outcome, but with Savino and Dimitri to back up the tall, blue-jawed Greek, the odds against him were far too high.

However, Larren was not the kind to sit back and die, and he was still determined to go down fighting. He knew that if he could change position and lose himself among the rocks he might still be able to take another of his enemies with him to oblivion, and hissing instructions to Andromavitch and Carla to remain where they were he began moving fast through the low rocks on his belly.

So far he had seen no sign of the man who had fired that single shot and he had no idea which of his enemies had caught up with him. But he reasoned that although the three Greeks would have spread out in order to locate him, they would now all be converging on the sanctuary in answer to that one shot.

The maze of scattered boulders offered plenty of cover, and Larren half crawled and half slithered in a sweeping half circle that took him away from the sea, preferring to carry the fight to his enemies rather than be cornered with his back to the cliff edge. Had it been possible he would have attempted to escape alone and sacrificed both Carla and Andromavitch in an effort to at least save the vital antidote. But he knew that it was too late for that now; it would take him too long to swing down the rope and he could be picked off with ease by a single shot as he dangled helplessly in space. And there was no other way of escape from Kyros.

Larren had lost sight of his companions now and he had no idea whether they were obeying his orders to remain motionless or not. Also he had still not located his unseen attacker in the rocks and he suddenly felt strangely and utterly alone. It was a curious sensation, but not wholly disturbing. Most of his life he had lived alone, and he had always expected to die alone. Everything around him seemed very still and silent and he moved with delicate care. Then abruptly his knee dislodged a handful of stones that rattled sharply into a shallow gulley beside him, and the sound instantly drew a second shot that ricocheted amid a shower of cracking splinters from a boulder just behind his left ear.

Larren dropped flat and in the same moment rolled half on to his left shoulder so that he could search to the right for his attacker.

He saw the man immediately, less than twenty yards away and rising slowly to his feet from behind a patch of scrub.

It was Savino.

Savino grinning broadly in the belief that he had wounded his target: Savino showing himself recklessly in his eagerness to avenge his damaged pride; Savino desperately eager to enjoy the glory of killing Larren alone before Christos and Dimitri could join him.

The handsome, youthful Greek was much too careless, and as he closed in, craving for a kill, Larren shot him once squarely through the chest.

The look of ecstasy drained from the handsome face and the features stiffened and then writhed, twisting more with shocked surprise than with pain. And then Savino slowly toppled backwards into the rocks.

Larren did not linger to taste the fierce elation that sprang up within him but instantly scrambled forwards to change his position. The inbred sixth sense of caution that moved him saved his life for within seconds of his departure a rifle bullet smacked viciously into the sand where he had been lying. As the report echoed through the rocks Larren dropped panting into a gulley that offered more complete cover and felt his moment of triumph vanish as swiftly as it had appeared. The sound of the rifle meant that Dimitri had reached the scene, and that Christos must be close behind. And these two men were neither hot heads, nor were they anxious to risk their lives in redeeming their pride. The death of Savino could not possibly be enough to affect the final outcome.

Slowly Larren inched his way along the gulley, knowing that Dimitri must have temporarily lost sight of him again and still determined to fight the issue to the end. His automatic was a poor match for the Greek's rifle but the maze of tumbled boulders would make accurate shooting from a distance almost impossible and he was not yet prepared to give up hope. There was still a chance that he would be able to kill another of his enemies before the resulting exchange of shots brought him his final bullet from the survivor.

He had not been able to mark down Dimitri's position when the man had taken that snap shot, but he knew that it hardly mattered, for the man was a professional and would have moved automatically. He also knew that by now Christos must have been attracted by the shooting, and although the area around the sanctuary seemed abruptly quiet and peaceful again he knew that he was playing a silent and deadly game of blind-man's-buff with two killers among the rocks.

The sun was very warm now and Larren was sweating freely. The palms of his hands were uncomfortably slippery again and he repeated his habitual movement of smoothing them down his thighs, deftly swapping his automatic from hand to hand as he did so. The spasm of alarm that had rushed through him when he had so narrowly escaped from Dimitri's rifle had left him now, and his nerve ends no longer jittered. He strained his ears without hearing any sound and wondered whether his opponents were closing in on him, or whether they were patiently waiting for him to move first.

He listened for a few moments longer and then decided that it was up to him to move. This time he made absolutely sure that there were no loose stones in his path that could roll and rattle from beneath his feet. He reached the end of the sheltering gulley and had to sink low on to his stomach again as he wriggled up over the edge. There was nothing before him except more boulders, sand and scrub. The only thing that moved was a three-inch lizard that suddenly ejected itself from the sand near his arm and scuttled swiftly away. Larren's stomach did a double somersault as it happened and then slowly subsided.

He swallowed hard and crawled on.

He covered another ten yards before sinking into a dark patch of shadow by a shoulder-high slab of rock, pausing there to regulate his rate of breathing and to listen. The stillness remained unbroken, and the savage terrain around him remained completely barren of human life. The lonely feeling of isolation had returned again, although he knew that the two Greeks had to be out there somewhere; either searching for him, or waiting for him.

Larren allowed his breathing to steady down and then warily continued his wriggling progress. His course was taking him further inland and he began to wonder whether it was possible that he had passed the two Greeks and was now heading away from them, and for a moment hope began to strengthen within him. While there was life there was always room for a tiny streak of hope, no matter how slender. If he could dodge this present issue then perhaps he would have time to find another way of escape from the island. And he would still have the antidote, even though he would have lost Andromavitch and Carla.

The encouraging thought stayed with him for perhaps three seconds.

Christos had been crouching low and motionless behind one of the many scattered boulders that littered the ground, watching coldly as Larren approached. He had emptied his automatic during the fighting at the beach and now he held a long, thin-bladed knife in his right hand. Larren was coming almost straight for him and when the British agent drew level Christos rose silently to his feet and sprang forwards.

But there was one factor that Christos

had been forced to leave to chance: the sun was behind him and threw his shadow ahead as he straightened up.

The falling shadow gave Larren a split second warning and he twisted desperately to avoid the murderous thrust of the knife, rolling backwards to face his attacker and jerking up the automatic in readiness to fire. Christos realized that he was going to miss and his descending body writhed in mid-air like the limbs of a cat struggling to find its feet as it fell. The direction of the knife thrust changed and the blade bit sharply into Larren's wrist as Christos aimed at his gun hand. The automatic shot from Larren's opened fingers as the Greek landed heavily beside him in the sand.

Larren continued his frenzied rolling, tumbling down a slight slope in his efforts to get clear of the knife. He came to his feet at the bottom with a nimble scrambling movement and swung back to face his enemy.

Christos was already upright, crouching and waiting. The blue stubble on his jaw was very pronounced now that he had gone overnight without shaving, and his light blue eyes had again taken on that hard dangerously-brittle look.

Larren's left hand moved inside his jacket, re-appeared holding his own knife, and then deftly transferred it to his right. The open gash on the back of his wrist gaped wider as his grip tightened and the blood spilled over his knuckles and dripped on to the ground. Larren tried not to look at it and swallowed the flood of nausea that came with the first rush of pain.

Christos began to circle to his left, coming gradually closer. He said softly, "This is the way it should be, Larren. Now we can settle what we started at the villa."

Larren wondered for a moment what had happened to Dimitri and he felt very vulnerable standing upright with his back exposed to any easy shot should the man appear behind him. But even so he felt another, stranger sensation of fulfilment. For he knew that Christos was right, and that deep down he too had wanted it to end in this way.

374

He too began to circle slowly, keeping the tall Greek in front of him all the time.

In the brief seconds before they became too close Larren had imprinted every rock and shrub in the vicinity with photographic detail into his memory, and now he knew exactly where to move to avoid tripping over backwards. Now his eyes never faltered in their steady gaze upon Christos's face. He could feel the blood still flowing from the cut across his wrist and he knew that he was losing too much and losing it too fast.

Christos said suddenly, calmly, "What happened to Savino?"

"He was over-eager," Larren answered in the same tone. "I think he was in too much hurry to avenge his pride."

"He is dead?"

"Yes."

It was impossible for those brittle eyes to become any harder, but the Greek's mouth twisted into an ugly line. He said nothing more but began to move his knife with slow, idle turns of his wrist. The sunlight caught the bright-edged point

375

of the slender blade in tiny flashes, but Larren knew better than to take his gaze from the Greek's face.

Christos moved with blinding speed, making a slashing feint towards Larren's throat, weaving back, feinting again and then dropping low on one knee to aim a long-armed thrust at the stomach. Larren was almost fooled by that second deceptive feint and it was mostly sheer instinct that caused him to twist sideways to the left to dodge that final thrust. The knife passed within an inch of his flinching stomach and the knuckles of the Greek's fist brushed his jacket. Desperately Larren grabbed the man's wrist before he could draw back and lunged his own blade at the exposed throat. Christos ducked frantically and threw up his left arm to deflect the blow. He threw himself backwards in the same moment and kicked one foot hard at Larren's crotch.

The kick landed a shade low on the inside of Larren's thigh and sent him staggering back. Christos landed heavily but was already springing lightly to his feet as Larren rushed him. Larren thrust towards the Greek's ribs and Christos instantly parried the blow, the two blades clanging together as the hilts locked. Desperately Larren's left hand came up again to grab the Greek's knife wrist and he swung his body round to shoulder charge the man solidly against the chest. They went down together and as they landed Larren swung his head sideways in a savage butting movement that brought his temple into violent contact with the Greek's nose. There was a crunching sound as the bone was smashed and Christos howled with pain.

Larren rolled to the left, lifting his weight from the Greek's body but still pinning down his right arm. He pulled back his own knife hand for the final thrust but Christos was still capable of fighting back. Larren choked with agony as a knee hit him solidly in the stomach and then Christos had grappled with him and was clinging feverishly to his knife wrist. Larren could feel himself weakening from the loss of blood and the new pain as the Greek's clawing fingers dug into his gashed wrist drove him mad with sudden fury. He tucked his chin down low and again butted his head viciously into Christos's face.

Christos was gasping harshly for breath now and the blood was spreading thickly across his face from his broken nose. But still he fought back, hanging wildly on to Larren's blood-drenched wrist and thrusting his knee in savage crippling blows to Larren's stomach. Then Larren made a frenzied effort to free his knife wrist and Christos's fingers slipped through the flowing blood. Larren leaned hard on the knife and saw Christos's mouth burst open with the rush of pain. The tall, struggling body beneath him seemed to recoil and stiffen, and then became still.

Larren got slowly to his knees, clutching at his injured wrist in effort to stop the bleeding and feeling very sick. He had to stay like that for a moment, but when he could focus his eyes again he saw that Christos was still breathing slightly and that the man's eyes were open.

The hard face smiled very thinly and he

croaked feebly, "So you were the better man, Larren, after all."

Larren knelt beside him and found that the savagery had drained away from them both. There was compassion in him now and he suddenly felt that he could well be watching himself die, or at least a part of himself. He remembered his own feeling that he and Christos were twins of the night; and Christos saying that they were brothers in blood. Now he had killed his brother and felt as tainted as Cain.

He said slowly, "But only just, Christos. Only just."

The brittle eyes had softened and the dying man had to force his last words out, his body shuddering slightly as he spoke.

"Do me one — one favour, Larren. Don't be too hard on Antonella."

Larren didn't understand. He said hoarsely, "What about Antonella?"

Christos did not hear. He stirred and said, "She was only doing it for her old man, Larren. Don't be too hard."

Larren stared at him stupidly and then realized that he was dead.

Slowly he stood up, trying to make sense out of Christos's words. His head was reeling and he couldn't think straight and he gave up after a few moments of puzzled effort. He stood staring down at Christos who lay sprawled on his back with the knife hilt standing upright just below his chest and felt an almost bitter taste of remorse in his throat. He and Christos had been enemies, but he felt more as though he had lost a friend.

He started to turn away, and then he heard a movement behind him. He remembered Dimitri and the rifle, but somehow it didn't seem to matter any more. He had never expected to get out of this alive anyway.

He turned round slowly, but it was not Dimitri who stepped out of the rocks to face him.

It was the slim young man with the figure of a ballet dancer; the man who called himself Adrian Cleyton.

20

Death on the Aegean

Larren could only think of one thing to say.

"Who the hell are you?"

Cleyton smiled. He was still wearing the soiled clothes he had found aboard the *Xenia*, but now they were soaked with sea water and were smelling even more highly of fish as they dried in the sun. He had an automatic in his hand but he showed no intention of using it. He said calmly, "We have a mutual friend, Larren. A man named Smith."

Larren became cautious. "I know a lot of Smiths."

Cleyton laughed. "This one has a book-lined office in Whitehall. On the left-hand side, fourth shelf from the bottom, there's a large volume on espionage throughout the ages which you were browsing through the last time you were there. Satisfied?"

Larren nodded, for the only man alive who could have known that he had shown an interest in that particular volume was Smith himself. He said slowly, "I'm satisfied, but I don't understand. I thought Smith had strict orders to leave this job alone."

"That's correct," Cleyton agreed. "But that was before Andromavitch vanished. When our scientist friend dodged security Smith had to find him. I was assigned the job of covering this end, and as it was pretty obvious that Valedri was tied in Smith had to explain to me about you. However, I had instructions to concentrate solely on Andromavitch and to leave you to your own job of getting the antidote; and once I saw that you had fallen foul of Valedri I followed instructions to the letter and simply kept you in sight from a distance. I was hoping that you might lead me to the man I was looking for, and you did, although it meant that I had to show my face and involve you with the police in order to save you from him."

Larren looked at the dead man beside

them and asked, "You mean Christos?"

"That's right. I can't prove it, but I'm pretty sure that it was your friend Christos who fixed Paolo Castel's car. Smith maintains contacts in most of the capital cities of the western world, and I got his man in Athens to check all arrivals and departures between Greece and Italy around the time Castel met with his so-called accident. He found that both Christos and his brother Savino made a trip to Milan four days before Castel died, and that they came back the day following. That could be a coincidence but I doubt it."

Larren remembered the photograph of Castel that he had taken from Savino and said, "You're undoubtedly right. Christos was an expert on sabotage in the Greek resistance during the war; he probably knew a dozen ways to booby-trap a car." Then he asked, "But how do you tie Christos to Andromavitch?"

"I didn't. As far as I know it was Valedri who wanted him, although I don't know why. But both jobs were so finely woven together somewhere that it seemed that my best bet was to stick to Christos and see what happened." He explained how he came to be aboard the *Xenia* and then finished up. "When Savino led his men ashore he left one man behind to deal with me, but the fellow was only expecting to find a simple fisherman when he came down into the cabin, and he was too confident to give me too much trouble. I swam ashore while the fighting was going on and then spotted our three friends chasing after you, so I tagged along."

Larren stiffened suddenly. "There's still one of them left," he exclaimed. "Christos's lieutenant is still wandering about with a rifle."

Cleyton shook his head. "He's finished wandering," he said smiling. "I left him unconscious in the rocks. He was so busy searching for you that the last thing he expected was to find an enemy behind him."

Larren had recovered a little now and he said grimly, "Even so, we had better get away from here before any more of those beauties on the beach decide to come exploring. I've got a launch below the cliffs and Andromavitch and Valedri's daughter are waiting above it."

Cleyton agreed readily, and Larren stopped only to bind up his cut wrist with a handkerchief that the younger man supplied before retrieving his knife and his automatic and leading the way back to the sanctuary. Andromavitch and Carla were still waiting behind the tall pinnacle of rock, and although the Russian waited for them to approach, Carla ran white-faced to meet them.

Larren cut short her frantic questions, introduced Cleyton simply as an unexpected friend, and insisted that there was still no time to properly explain. He over-rode Andromavitch's demands equally roughly and told the old man that now that Cleyton was here to descend the cliff first and bring the launch over to the rope there would be no more difficulty in getting them all down.

Cleyton accepted the task without argument and swung nimbly over the edge of the cliff. They watched him reach the end of the rope and drop into the sea, and then a few seconds later he reappeared on the surface and swam strongly towards the launch.

Without any further delay Larren hauled the rope up and knotted the end into a large loop in which Carla could sit as he lowered her down. His wrist was throbbing now and he ordered the reluctant Andromavitch to help him pass the rope over the edge of the cliff. When the rope was fully paid out Carla slipped out of her seat and tumbled clumsily into the sea within a few feet of the launch, and almost immediately Cleyton hauled her aboard.

Larren pulled the rope up again and turned to Andromavitch.

The muscles in the Russian's face worked undecidedly, and then he burst out abruptly, "I still refuse to go. It is too risky, and with that injured hand you are liable to let go of the rope."

Larren looked into the man's face, and something about the undefinable colour of the eyes played a chord in his mind. He looked up to that mane of ginger-red, almost bronze-red hair, and quite suddenly a lot of things became clear.

He pulled out his automatic, pointed it calmly at the blustering scientist and said grimly, "I think perhaps you're right about not going. You're not going anywhere."

Andromavitch stared. "What — what does this mean?"

"It means that I've tumbled to the obvious. It was a good try, Professor, and you almost pulled it off. But it was a pity that your own daughter double-crossed you."

The Russian's fleshy face jerked convulsively. "I — I do not understand," he struggled weakly.

"You understand all right. I should have guessed the moment I saw that red hair and the colour of your eyes, except that I was too busy to think straight, and even when Christos told me outright the truth still didn't register. But it has now. The girl who calls herself Antonella is your daughter; the one who was supposed to have drowned during a moonlight swimming party outside Athens."

Andromavitch said nothing and Larren went on.

"It's all beginning to fit now. I couldn't understand what Valedri wanted with a nuclear scientist; but the answer is that he didn't want you at all. Nobody wanted you. It was you who wanted to get away. I think it must have been you who planned the death of Paolo Castel, knowing that Valedri could then be seduced by Antonella into using the Ameytheline antidote for blackmail purposes and also into naming you as part of the price. No doubt you thought that the British Government would release you without question rather than allow the red death to continue, and you could then vanish without trace with part of the blackmail money. Isn't that right, Professor?"

Andromavitch did not trouble to deny it. Savage anger had smoothed away his first reactions and he blazed furiously, "Of course it is right. I wanted my freedom, don't you understand. *My Freedom!* All my life all that I have ever wanted is simply to be free. But no! That is not possible. Because I am intelligent — because I have a superior brain — because I can understand nuclear physics better than any man alive — because of all these things I am not allowed to be free. I am no more than a prize animal who must be watched and guarded day and night. Every hour of my life there has always been the shadow of a security man behind me. Everywhere I go that shadow always follows. In Russia it was the secret police, the K.G.B., always following, always watching. And so I waited my chance and fled to the West, the glorious, unchained, unfettered freedom of the West. And what did I find. I find that freedom is only for the lower species. For the scientist — for the prize animal — there must always be policemen in the shadows. They tell me that it is for my own protection, because the Russians might try to kidnap me back. Just as in Russia it was for my own protection in case the British or the Americans should try to steal me away. I am sick of it! I am an old man and all that I want is to be free."

Larren said harshly, "And you didn't

mind using the red death to achieve that freedom?"

"You think that I should!" Andromavitch was raging with contempt. He touched his broad forehead and tapped it violently. "Here I have the knowledge to wipe out whole cities; to destroy whole nations. Do you think that a few isolated deaths from a simple drug should mean anything to a man like me?"

Larren made no answer and the old man rushed on, "When I learned that Ameytheline was a killer I saw the opportunity that I have been searching for all my life — the opportunity to escape. I knew that if I simply tried to vanish I wouldn't have had a hope of succeeding, for I should have had every intelligence agent in Western Europe swarming at my heels. The only way was to employ some threat that would ensure that they did not dare attempt to find me. And the use of the Ameytheline antidote supplied the perfect answer.

"I had plenty of time to perfect my plans, for I had friends in medical circles who knew the facts long before the story was discovered by the newspapers. The first victims of the red death were the laboratory workers who had volunteered themselves as guinea pigs when the drug was being tested, and although the existing supplies of Ameytheline were immediately frozen, the facts were somehow hushed up until the deaths began to occur among the general public months later. During this time Castel was already working hard to find the antidote, and I was working on the best way of using it once he succeeded.

"I made discreet inquiries and found out that Castel was unmarried, and that his next of kin was his father. Angelo Valedri. The mere fact that an ex-jailbird with a grudge against society would become the legal owner of Castel's effects if the boy was to die suggested possibilities, and I sent Antonella to investigate more deeply. The result was more rewarding than I had dared to hope, for Valedri became infatuated with her, and once I realized that he would do practically anything she asked I was able to make definite plans.

"Antonella faked her own death and became Valedri's mistress, and within weeks she had completely gained his sympathy for me. She played upon the fact that we had both been persecuted in our different ways by the society he hated. And by the time Castel had perfected the antidote I knew that I only had to arrange an accident that would not arouse Valedri's suspicions, and then Antonella would have no difficulty in persuading the old fool to make the blackmail demand as I had planned it.

"I still had my contacts in the medical world, and I was able to keep myself up to date on Castel's progress. When I knew he was on the point of success I warned Antonella who had already hired a man named Christos to take care of the accident. The plan was that Christos should keep constant watch on Castel in the final stages, and then kill him as soon as he perfected the antidote. The antidote samples and any relevant notes were to be posted to Valedri, together with a cleverly forged note that would appear to have been written by Castel himself. The note stated that Castel had learned by chance about his father, and wanted him to take care of the samples because he didn't fully trust his associates in Milan."

Andromavitch stopped, and there was a brief moment of silence.

Then Larren said slowly, "But you made one miscalculation, didn't you? You under-estimated your own importance. You didn't get a chance to make a gallant show of giving yourself up to stop the plague, because the Government hushed up the facts about both the antidote, and the blackmail demand."

Andromavitch nodded. "I think I knew then that I could never present them with a big enough crisis to cause them to willingly release me, but I felt that I had to see the thing through to the limit. I escaped from my guards and left a note saying that I had learned the truth directly from Valedri and that I was giving myself up exactly as he had asked. I hoped that once I had taken matters into my own hands they would give way and accept the antidote in exchange."

Larren said, "But you were unlucky.

Antonella had fallen in love with Christos and that caused too many complications. It's obvious that Christos didn't realize exactly what he was handling when he posted the antidote to Valedri, but he did find out afterwards, or else Antonella told him, and he determined to get it back and cut himself in on the blackmail money. I imagine that he had to promise Antonella that you would not suffer, and that he would simply be taking Valedri's place."

Larren was suddenly certain that the launch that Christos had warned away from the beach-front villa must have carried Antonella, and he went on grimly, "Christos and Antonella did their best to kidnap Carla in the hope of forcing Valedri to relinquish both you and the antidote. But I spoiled that, so Christos decided to take everything by force. Everything got so mixed up when you landed on Kyros that you must have been glad to see a British agent again."

Andromavitch looked up slowly, his eyes filled with hate.

"No, Larren!" He said harshly. "If I had realized what was going on I would have tried to reach Antonella and Christos and taken my chances with them. I wish Christos had killed you!"

They faced each other in cold silence, and then Andromavitch smiled thinly.

"So now you know, Larren. But I don't think that you can do anything about it. You say that you have the antidote, and I don't doubt that you had to kill Angelo Valedri to get it. Christos is also dead, and that only leaves Antonella who knows the truth. And Antonella is a highly intelligent girl who is devoted to me. She is safe with Christos's men and she will realize that she has only to disappear again and no one will ever be able to prove that she did not drown at that swimming party. It will be my word against yours, Larren, and you don't have a shred of evidence to back you up. You can drag me back to London but you will never be able to bring a case against me. I have a reputation and influence, and my tracks are too well covered. Besides, I have the hero's role; when the newspapers learn how I attempted to sacrifice myself in exchange for the antidote I shall have the gratitude of the country." Andromavitch's smile became fully confident. "I am quite happy to go back to London with you, Larren. I shall deny this conversation and enjoy watching you make a fool of yourself when you try to prove otherwise."

Larren laughed softly. "You're miscalculating again, Professor. You underestimated your own importance — and now you're under-estimating me. I'm not interested in taking you back to London. I'm a lone operator, and I have no scruples about proving anything to anybody. I'm quite happy to act as judge, jury — and executioner. That's why I sent Cleyton down to the launch out of the way. He might not have agreed."

For a moment fear showed in those undefinable eyes, and then it was gone. The old man braced himself and said, "Perhaps I have found my freedom."

Larren nodded slowly, and then he raised the automatic in his hand and fired once.

Andromavitch did not even flinch. His large body simply sagged with the impact, and then he closed his eyes and fell.

He had died instantly.

* * *

When Larren reached the launch he told Cleyton that Andromavitch had been killed by a lucky shot from a second party of Christos's men coming up from the beach. The slim man cursed him furiously for a bungling fool, but Larren used the same lie as an excuse to ignore him and get the launch speeding out into the Aegean.

Carla came up to stand beside him, but now that the danger was over he could not face her any more and he was glad when she turned away. He had used her, and he had murdered her father, and now that he realized that Valedri had been just an old man, twenty years out of date, who had been used by everyone around him, he was no longer proud of his achievements.

The sun had climbed higher in the sky and was burning down savagely as Kyros dropped away behind them. The heat made Larren dizzy, and when he looked down at the blood seeping through the white handkerchief round his wrist he felt suddenly sick. He had seen too much blood and killed too many times in the past few days. He swayed unsteadily at the wheel and then Cleyton took over and told him curtly to sit down. Carla helped him into the cabin and on to the bunk, and he wished fervently that she would leave him alone.

Carefully he checked that the two phials of the Ameytheline antidote were still safe and unbroken in the breast pocket of his shirt. All he had to do was to pass those phials on to Smith, and with Valedri in no position to complain the British Government could blandly announce that their own chemists had made the discovery.

It was all so easy now that Larren felt quite justified in passing out.

A FOOT IN THE GRAVE
Bruce Marshall

About to be imprisoned and tortured in Buenos Aires, John Smith escapes, only to become involved in an aeroplane hijacking.

DEAD TROUBLE
Martin Carroll

Trespassing brought Jennifer Denning more than she bargained for. She was totally unprepared for the violence which was to lie in her path.

HOURS TO KILL
Ursula Curtiss

Margaret went to New Mexico to look after her sick sister's rented house and felt a sharp edge of fear when the absent landlady arrived.

THE DEATH OF ABBE DIDIER
Richard Grayson

Inspector Gautier of the Sûreté investigates three crimes which are strangely connected.

NIGHTMARE TIME
Hugh Pentecost

Have the missing major and his wife met with foul play somewhere in the Beaumont Hotel, or is their disappearance a carefully planned step in an act of treason?

BLOOD WILL OUT
Margaret Carr

Why was the manor house so oddly familiar to Elinor Howard? Who would have guessed that a Sunday School outing could lead to murder?

THE DRACULA MURDERS
Philip Daniels

The Horror Ball was interrupted by a spectral figure who warned the merrymakers they were tampering with the unknown.

THE LADIES
OF LAMBTON GREEN
Liza Shepherd

Why did murdered Robin Colquhoun's picture pose such a threat to the ladies of Lambton Green?

CARNABY
AND THE GAOLBREAKERS
Peter N. Walker

Detective Sergeant James Aloysius Carnaby-King is sent to prison as bait. When he joins in an escape he is thrown headfirst into a vicious murder hunt.

MUD IN HIS EYE
Gerald Hammond

The harbourmaster's body is found mangled beneath Major Smyle's yacht. What is the sinister significance of the illicit oysters?

THE SCAVENGERS
Bill Knox

Among the masses of struggling fish in the *Tecta*'s nets was a larger, darker, ominously motionless form . . . the body of a skin diver.

DEATH IN ARCADY
Stella Phillips

Detective Inspector Matthew Furnival works unofficially with the local police when a brutal murder takes place in a caravan camp.

STORM CENTRE
Douglas Clark

Detective Chief Superintendent Masters, temporarily lecturing in a police staff college, finds there's more to the job than a few weeks relaxation in a rural setting.

THE MANUSCRIPT MURDERS
Roy Harley Lewis

Antiquarian bookseller Matthew Coll, acquires a rare 16th century manuscript. But when the Dutch professor who had discovered the journal is murdered, Coll begins to doubt its authenticity.

SHARENDEL
Margaret Carr

Ruth didn't want all that money. And she didn't want Aunt Cass to die. But at Sharendel things looked different. She began to wonder if she had a split personality.

MURDER TO BURN
Laurie Mantell

Sergeants Steven Arrow and Lance Brendon, of the New Zealand police force, come upon a woman's body in the water. When the dead woman is identified they begin to realise that they are investigating a complex fraud.

YOU CAN HELP ME
Maisie Birmingham

Whilst running the Citizens' Advice Bureau, Kate Weatherley is attacked with no apparent motive. Then the body of one of her clients is found in her room.

DAGGERS DRAWN
Margaret Carr

Stacey Manston was the kind of girl who could take most things in her stride, but three murders were something different . . .

THE MONTMARTRE MURDERS
Richard Grayson

Inspector Gautier of Sûreté investigates the disappearance of artist Théo, the heir to a fortune.

GRIZZLY TRAIL
Gwen Moffat

Miss Pink, alone in the Rockies, helps in a search for missing hikers, solves two cruel murders and has the most terrifying experience of her life when she meets a grizzly bear!

BLINDMAN'S BLUFF
Margaret Carr

Kate Deverill had considered suicide. It was one way out — and preferable to being murdered.

BEGOTTEN MURDER
Martin Carroll

When Susan Phillips joined her aunt on a voyage of 12,000 miles from her home in Melbourne, she little knew their arrival would germinate the seeds of murder planted long ago.

WHO'S THE TARGET?
Margaret Carr

Three people whom Abby could identify as her parents' murderers wanted her dead, but she decided that maybe Jason could have been the target.

THE LOOSE SCREW
Gerald Hammond

After a motor smash, Beau Pepys and his cousin Jacqueline, her fiancé and dotty mother, suspect that someone had prearranged the death of their friend. But who, and why?

CASE WITH THREE HUSBANDS
Margaret Erskine

Was it a ghost of one of Rose Bonner's late husbands that gave her old Aunt Agatha such a terrible shock and then murdered her in her bed?

THE END OF THE RUNNING
Alan Evans

Lang continued to push the men and children on and on. Behind them were the men who were hunting them down, waiting for the first signs of exhaustion before they pounced.

CARNABY AND THE HIJACKERS
Peter N. Walker

When Commander Pigeon assigns Detective Sergeant Carnaby-King to prevent a raid on a bullion-carrying passenger train, he knows that there are traitors in high positions.

TREAD WARILY AT MIDNIGHT
Margaret Carr

If Joanna Morse hadn't been so hasty she wouldn't have been involved in the accident.

TOO BEAUTIFUL TO DIE
Martin Carroll

There was a grave in the churchyard to prove Elizabeth Weston was dead. Alive, she presented a problem. Dead, she could be forgotten. Then, in the eighth year of her death she came back. She was beautiful, but she had to die.

IN COLD PURSUIT
Ursula Curtiss

In Mexico, Mary and her cousin Jenny each encounter strange men, but neither of them realises that one of these men is obsessed with revenge and murder. But which one?

LITTLE DROPS OF BLOOD
Bill Knox

It might have been just another unfortunate road accident but a few little drops of blood pointed to murder.

GOSSIP TO THE GRAVE
Jonathan Burke

Jenny Clark invented Simon Sherborne because her daily gossip column was getting dull. Then Simon appeared at a party — in the flesh! And Jenny finds herself involved in murder.

HARRIET FAREWELL
Margaret Erskine

Wealthy Theodore Buckler had planned a magnificent Guy Fawkes Day celebration. He hadn't planned on murder.